Hunter

Edna!
Go Bloodhounds!
"Class of '54"

By Jerry Hooten

Jerry Hooten

i

ISBN-13: 978-1463734404

ISBN-10: 1463734409

Chapter 1

Jeff shook hands with Conrad Erikson, the CEO of Erikson International. Erikson International dealt in small arms for police and some government agencies.

"I think you will be very pleased with this new system. All the components are state of the art and have been proven in the field."

Erikson smiled as he walked with Jeff in the warehouse. "I just hope we never have the need for it. I would prefer that we have no incident that requires it."

Jeff agreed. Most of the systems that Hunter Security employed were designed as a deterrent. Their reputation was one of the best in the field and having a "Hunter Security" placard on a business was a big deterrent in itself.

"You'll be able to sleep nights, knowing this system and our company is protecting your assets."

"Thanks again, I hope our relationship works well for both of us." Erikson squeezed Jeff's shoulder as Jeff exited the building and headed towards his car. They waved as Jeff put the car in gear and headed out the main gate of the perimeter fencing. The guard at the gate waved from his site at the guard shack. The gate closed behind Jeff as he headed towards the highway.

Erikson International was located on 200 acres of land just outside of the city. The entire facility had been fenced off with eight foot galvanized fencing with rolled razor wire topping. The fence itself was electronically monitored for any attempt to gain entry, and the ground between the fence and the building was guarded with seismic sensors. All of the buildings were outfitted with night vision video cameras that also were equipped with video motion sensors. Anything moving on the grounds would set off an alarm and activate the video recording to real time. All the cameras, 24 of them in all, were recorded in time lapse by streaming video to a server onsite as well as at the Hunter Security main office. In accordance with the contract, Hunter Security kept surveillance with the facility along with the company security guards on site.

Jeff was very pleased with the system as a whole. The only concern he had was that the company hired their own security guards and did their own background checks. He preferred to do the hiring himself, but it was their prerogative to hire their own if they so chose.

The installation had started with the construction of the facility and now it was completed. It was quite a plum for Hunter Security. Maybe they could get some of the new monitoring computers they wanted now.

It was a bright sunny day. Traffic was light on the two-lane highway. Jeff had dressed up wearing dress pants and a tie to go with his usual sport coat. He loosened the tie as he drove back to the office. Since he was already half way cleaned up, he thought he'd ask his partner and fiancée, MJ out to dinner. It would be a good night to celebrate. He hadn't talked to her before he left the office this morning. She had been on another assignment, meeting with the agent of a rock star for providing some body guard work.

Things were good. Maybe if business stayed good, they could move their wedding date up. They had been engaged for four years and living together the last year. Financially, they were ready, and emotionally, they had been ready since they first met. It had been love at first sight for both of them. Quarrels were few and far between, and the making up had made the quarrels worth it in the end.

Jeff had to grin at that thought. Maybe he could start a quarrel so they could make up again.

Chapter 2

MJ rolled her eyes. Not so the agent could see them, but she was just about to the point of being fed up with his efforts to impress her with his importance. True, he had a talented young singer for a client, but that was more luck than expertise on his part.

They had agreed that Hunter Security would provide the singer with bodyguards during his stay for the two night performances he had scheduled. They would escort him from the airport to the hotel and then to the coliseum and keep fans away from his dressing room and vehicle. It was pretty basic escort service really. MJ already had the personnel picked for the job, two ex-policemen that worked for them on a will-call basis. They'd be well paid and the job would be a breeze for them. They had done this same kind of service for them for years.

"Thanks again for thinking of us Mr. Krug." MJ shook his sweaty, limp hand and headed for the exit. They had met at the coffee shop in the hotel where Krug was making arrangements for the group to stay. She could feel his eyes wandering over her as she headed away. Such a creep!

When she got to the car, she put the briefcase with the contract in the back seat, then got into the front seat and pulled out her cell phone. She called in and had Marty, the secretary, call Roger and Kelly with the information about the job. They'd get together later this afternoon to work out the details. Roger and Kelly had worked together before and knew the routine. It should be a piece of cake.

She put the phone back in her purse after checking for messages. She'd had one from Jeff, checking to see about dinner. She'd call him back from the office, unless he beat her there.

She checked traffic, then pulled out from the curb and headed back to the strip mall where their office was located. Dinner tonight sounded like a plan.

Chapter3

Jeff pulled in the parking in front of the office. He saw that MJ's car was already there. He parked the Spectra and stepped out of the car. He got his sport coat out of the back seat and put it on while he was walking towards the office. He clicked the remote, locking the car, then went in the office.

Marty looked up as he entered. "Hi boss, MJ just signed a contract with Rebel Yell."

"Super! Who's going to be on the job?"

"Kelly and Roger."

"That sounds good, have you talked to them yet?" Jeff stopped to check through the incoming mail.

"Got them both. They're coming in later for a meet with MJ"

Marty waved at Jeff and picked up the phone to answer an incoming call. Jeff headed back towards his office. He wanted to go over the contract with Erikson International before he gave it to Marty to enter in the system. He stopped by MJ's office on the way. She was leaning over the file cabinet to get some papers when he looked in. He admired the view of her well-shaped rear.

"Nice!" he said and grinned when MJ looked up, her face a little red, either from the comment, or the exertion, he wasn't sure which.

MJ grinned back. "You should know. Say, dinner sounds great. How about let's trying that new restaurant down the street. Everybody says it's just great."

"Works for me. I hear you got Rebel Yell signed up. Good job. I finalized the contract with Erikson this morning too. We're batting a thousand!"

"Good time to celebrate. Let's do it before something happens and screws up our plans." MJ slid behind her desk and laid the paperwork in front of her. "I've got to get the contracts for Roger and Kelly ready, and then I'll be ready for a quick lunch. How about you?"

Jeff checked the mail in his hand. "Not much here, give me ten and I'll be ready."

Jeff turned and walked down the short aisle to his office. He tossed the mail on his desk and hung his jacket on the hall tree in the corner. He pulled the contract with Erikson out of his briefcase and put it next to the mail. First things first.

He opened the contract and did a quick cursory over the pages. He'd already checked this several times over the past few months. Everything looked in order. He put the contract in his outbox for Marty and turned to the mail. Marty weeded out the regular office mail, bills, invoices and such. She handled most of that, sorting out which went to Jeff and what went to MJ. She would have the checks written out for payment and ready for their signatures. Marty was a great asset. Jeff made a mental note to see about getting her a raise. The business could afford it, and she had certainly earned it. He would discuss it with MJ over lunch.

The last letter in the bunch looked like a personal note. It was addressed to him in ink, with no return address. He opened the envelope and took out a lined page from a notebook. He unfolded it to find a handwritten note that at first, he thought was a joke. It said simply, "You're going to get yours!" No signature, no heading. He barked a short laugh. Somebody's idea of a joke?

Just to be on the safe side, he handled the sheet of paper by the corners and slid it into a clear plastic envelope. He kept them as evidence bags, but seldom ever used them. He'd have Marty get a fingerprint check and file a report with the police. Better safe than sorry.

This would be another item for discussion with MJ at lunch. He taped a short post it note to Marty on the bag. She'd take care of the rest of it.

He checked over the rest of the mail and put it all in his outbox for Marty. He grabbed his sport coat from the rack and shrugged into it as he left the office and headed down to get MJ for their lunch date.

MJ was ready and standing at the door to her office. He couldn't help but give her a look over. She looked good enough for lunch. She had on a black business suit with a collared blouse. An old F.B.I. lapel pin was in the jacket of her suit. Her dark brown hair was swept back in her usual pony tail. She wore a pair of diamond studs in her ears and looked gorgeous. Jeff thought he was the luckiest man on the planet!

He put an arm around MJ's shoulders as she slid hers around his waist. They smiled into each others eyes and walked down the short aisle, bumping hips at every opportunity. Marty looked up and laughed. "You're just going out for lunch, right?"

Jeff and MJ exchanged a look. "Right! Just lunch. We'll be back within an hour."

They were all laughing as Jeff and MJ headed out the door.

Chapter 4

They had lunch at the Subway a few blocks from the office. It was a nice day, and they had walked the short distance. MJ was telling Jeff about the agent she had met that morning.

"I really don't see how a nice kid like Donnie got mixed up with an agent like Krug. He gives me the creeps." Donnie was the lead singer with Rebel Yell; Donnie Young was his full name.

"Krug seems to know the business; you have to give him that." Jeff washed down the last of his sandwich with a big drink of green tea. MJ had opted for just a salad. She had a workout coming up later in the afternoon.

"I know, but he still gives me the creeps, after a session with him, I feel violated."

Jeff grinned, "Hey, that's my department. Maybe I should talk to him."

MJ punched him in the arm, not too lightly. "We'll see who violates whom tonight!"

"Promises, promises," Jeff said, rubbing his arm, "Good English!" he added, laughing.

They finished lunch and headed back to the office. As they walked in the door, Marty looked up.

"Jeff, Captain Harris called, said it was important."

"Thanks Marty, I'll call him right now." Jeff and MJ went into their respective offices. Jeff hung up his jacket and picked up the phone. He dialed the police captain's number from memory. They kept in touch quite often. Jeff was on their list of SME's, or subject matter experts for questions regarding security issues.

"Captain John. Jeff Hunter here, how can I be of assistance?"

"Jeff, glad you called. We have a problem that maybe you can help us with." John Harris was the shift captain at the police department. "We've had a string of break-ins, and whoever is doing it knows his stuff."

"How so?" Jeff asked.

"Well, first off, he's bypassed every alarm system prior to breaking in. Not just a matter of cutting a phone

13

line either. Some of the systems had a cellular backup and he's managed to block them too."

Jeff was interested. This wasn't some smash and grab druggie. You had to know your stuff to bypass a cellular backup system.

"Sounds like you've got a pro on your hands. How can I help?"

"If you could, I'd like for you to see this latest B&E. We're not getting much in the way of leads." Harris sounded concerned over the phone. Jeff could visualize his friend, running his hand over his bald head.

"I've got some time now. You want to meet at the site?"

"That would be great." Harris gave Jeff the address and they made arrangements to meet at the site of the burglary.

Jeff grabbed his coat off the hook and headed out of the office. "I'm meeting Captain Harris at 3950 Collinsville Road Marty. I should be back in a couple of hours at the most."

Marty wrote down the address and waved at Jeff. The phone was ringing as he stepped out of the office and headed towards his car.

Chapter 5

Jeff drove towards the address that Harris had provided. He remembered that it was a small jewelry store, part of a chain that was headquartered out of state. He knew that they did their security with a nationwide company that offered cheaper deals on security than he could provide. He also knew that you got what you paid for when it came to security.

Jeff pulled into a spot in front of the store. Captain Harris's vehicle was parked next to him, a typical cop car, a Crown Vic. It was unmarked, but with the plain wheels and antennas, it was easy to spot.

Harris was standing at the front door. He must have just arrived.

"Good timing" he said as Jeff got out of his car. "I just got here myself."

"Hey John, how's things."

"Could be better. This is the tenth store this month. All the same M.O. This guy is good, doesn't leave us much to work with." Harris held the door and Jeff preceded him into the jewelry store.

A small man in a dark suit, wearing a red bowtie watched them enter. He was wringing his hands and nodding, as though he was expecting them.

Harris introduced the man as Mr. Brownell, the manager of the store. Brownell was as bald as Harris, and you could see little beads of sweat on his forehead. Jeff thought he looked like he was ready for a breakdown.

"Mr. Brownell, I'm sorry to hear about your trouble. I'm here to help the police with their investigation." Brownell gave Jeff a quick, nervous handshake and motioned them toward the rear of the store.

They went through an open doorway and into the rear of the store. There were two large safes on the floor, their doors standing open. Jeff looked at the back door. It had some obvious damage around the deadbolt and doorknob.

"A repair man is on his way, they smashed their way into the store through that door." Brownell motioned to the obvious. Jeff noticed that there were

17

magnetic contacts on the door. The alarm keypad was next to the door.

"Was the alarm disabled?" Jeff asked. "I'm assuming there was an entrance and exit delay. How long did you have to disable the alarm, and how much time did you have to exit after it was armed?"

"It had a thirty second entrance and exit delay. The panel itself is in that closet over there." Brownell pointed to a small door on the opposite side of the room. "It is the mechanical closet, actually. Our telephone service and electrical service are there, along with the water and gas meters."

"Do the meter readers go into the closet to read the meters?" Jeff asked, knowing the probable answer. He was proved right when Brownell stated that the meters had remote readers. The water meter sent it's readings out over the telephone line at a preset time, and the gas meter was read with a proximity reader that allowed the meter reader to get the readings without even leaving his vehicle. It was a pretty standard procedure, but he had to check. Jeff wanted to know who had access to the interior of the shop and how much access they had. "Do you keep it locked?"

"Yes, the closet is always locked unless there is any maintenance that needs to be done. We don't use it for storage or any other purpose." Brownell was still wringing his hands. He made Jeff nervous just watching him.

"When was the last time you had any maintenance men in there?" Jeff went over to take a look as Brownell went over to unlock the closet door.

"About a month ago, the telephone man was here. We had another phone system installed. Our old system was the old type phones and we changed over to cordless phones."

Jeff looked around the small room. The alarm panel was on the wall next to the telephone demark point. The gas and water meters were on the wall opposite, near the floor. Jeff could see the cellular antenna attached to the top of the alarm panel. The alarm company logo was on the panel. It had a simple key lock on the panel door. There were several holes drilled through the front of the panel door. The cover had been pried open and the battery backup was disconnected.

Harris spoke for the first time since they had come to this back room.

"The alarm never reached the central station. There is an external siren that had been jammed and the wires to it were cut. The telephone lines were cut. It couldn't have been easy; all the wiring came out of the roof. There were signs that maybe an extension ladder had been leaned against the back wall. The outdoor lights behind the building had been shot out with a pellet gun. When Brownell came to open this morning, the door was still standing partially open, the lock broken. The alarm panel was dead. The keypad was dark. Both safes were standing open and the high value items from the safe were missing."

Harris pointed to the open safes. Several of the inner doors showed signs of being pried open. The vault doors showed that they had been drilled between the combination knob and the handle.

"What I don't get is why the cellular backup didn't kick in. It should have started the minute the outside lines were cut. There is a telephone monitor built into the system that activates the cellular as soon as the telephone line shows a voltage drop. The central station said they didn't receive any calls, either from the alarm itself or anything through the cellular." Brownell was nodding in agreement with Harris, who was rubbing his head again. No wonder he was bald.

Jeff looked at the alarm panel again. Whoever had drilled it knew where to put the holes. The panel itself would have taken the biggest hit. It didn't look like the cellular link had been hit at all. Someone had pulled the power from it after the panel damage.

"They had to have used a cell jammer." Jeff was examining the cell backup. "The cell itself appears to be o.k. It was disconnected after they got inside and ruined the panel."

"What's a cell jammer?" Brownell and Harris spoke at the same time.

"A cell jammer is a radio device that transmits on the same frequency that cell phones use to communicate to the towers. They vary in power, some have a limited range of a few feet, and others can block a large area. The cell phone usually just displays a 'no service', and both incoming and outgoing calls are blocked. Some churches and universities are using them

21

to maintain an atmosphere free of cell phone interruptions." Jeff examined the antenna on the alarm panel. "Another way is to ground out the transmitting antenna. You can sometimes stick a pin or other sharp object into an antenna and short the inner conductor to ground." He finished his examination. "That didn't happen here, there are no marks on the antenna, and besides, it would have transmitted an alarm before anybody got close enough to short it out."

"How big is this jammer, and how did they get it here, and how did they know there was a cell backup on the alarm?" Harris was looking over the antenna that Jeff had just examined.

"Some of the low power units aren't much bigger than a cell phone themselves," Jeff explained, "Other, more powerful units could easily be operated from a car or van, using the car battery as a power source. They could shut down all cell phone service in the entire block."

Just then, the repairman arrived to fix the door. He and Brownell went to examine the door and frame. Harris and Jeff went over to look at the safes.

Jeff looked closely at the first safe. "It looks like they used the 'weak point drilling' system to bypass the lock. Notice that both safes were drilled in the same location." Jeff pointed at the holes that were drilled in each safe. "Weak points are used by locksmiths when the safe's owner forgets or loses the combination. That information is a closely guarded secret in both the manufacturer's and the locksmiths' bag of tricks. You don't find them on newer safes. These babies are really old." Jeff pointed at the old faded floral pattern painted on the door of the safe. "I'd say these are probably almost a hundred years old."

Brownell had come over to join them. "You guessed right, Mr. Hunter. We have new safes on order. We were planning on moving our business into the mall. The president of the company didn't think it would be cost effective to pay the expense of moving the new safes, so we were planning on getting rid of these when we moved." He patted the top of the safe, "These have been here since before I started working here twenty years ago. The previous manager told me that they dated back to the 1800's."

The safes were impressive in looks, even if they weren't all that secure. The inner doors were just a light gauge metal and had been pried open. The simple locks on them would have been no problem to bypass. All the doors were open now. The only contents were some papers in the top right hand compartment.

The crime scene crew had dusted everything for fingerprints. One of the crew had already printed the employees to eliminate their prints from any of the burglars.

"How many people do you think were involved in this, Jeff?" Harris was looking around the scene.

"Probably at least two or three." Jeff said, "One in the vehicle, as a getaway driver and operating the cell jammer, one or two to bypass the alarm and do the actual break-in. Two at the very least, but I'd think they'd have a look-out posted on the street out front too, just to be safe. These guys didn't take too many chances."

"The other break-ins were similar, but not exactly the same." Harris said, "Several of the others just had

24

the locks picked or bypassed. Usually it was merchandise that was on display. We had a couple of electronics stores, several liquor stores, and a couple of pharmacies." Harris was running his hand over his head again. "All had alarms, four of them with cell backups."

"Diverse bunch of crooks. They have to have someplace to peddle all this stuff." Jeff and Harris walked into the front of the store. There were two employees there, being interviewed by the detective working the case.

"Why did they smash the doors here, instead of just picking the locks?" Harris leaned back on one of the empty display cases.

"Good locks here, was probably the main reason. I noticed both the door locks and the dead bolts were Medco high security locks. Would have taken a lot of skill and time to pick those, along with some special picks. Easier to just bust in. Not much traffic in back there, and with the lights out, it would be even less noticeable. This store is pretty remote from any residential area, not too many people around in the middle of the night."

Harris nodded his agreement. They headed back out to the cars. Harris stopped to exchange a few words with the detective, and then joined Jeff at the cars. Harris followed Jeff back to Hunter Security.

Harris powered down his window. "I got a call, I have to head back to the station.

Jeff nodded and walked over to Harris. "You might want to check with the wireless folks to see if they've had any reports of outages in the area. You might be able to pinpoint the time and how much of an area was shut down."

Harris was writing in his notebook as Jeff went on.

"Whoever did this was a locksmith at some point in time. If you get a suspect, that might be something to look for. Locksmiths have to be registered. I think the jammer was probably a fairly high power job too. It would probably be mounted in whatever vehicle they're using for the jobs."

Harris finished writing and held his hand out to Jeff. "Thanks for the info Jeff. I'll be in touch if we find anything. You might want to crank up the security on your accounts. Let me know if any of yours get hit. We've warned the other security companies in town."

"If I think of anything else, I'll give you a call John. Thanks for the heads up."

Jeff waved at the Captain as he drove off and went into the office. Marty was waiting for him.

"Jeff, got a call from Mr. Erikson, of Erikson International, he had a list of the employees that are his security personnel. He had their background checks, pictures, ta da, ta da, I had him fax them to us. I put them in your office in your in-box."

"Thanks Marty. I'll go over them and get them back to you so you can file them with the account information."

Jeff went to his office, pulled his jacket off and hung it on the tree. He took the folder out of his in-box with the Erikson info in it and laid it on his desk. He wanted to personally check each employee to make sure they met his criteria. He could give his estimation to Erikson and then it would be up to Erikson to make the final decision if there were any problems.

Most of the files were pretty thorough. He set three aside for further consideration. He picked up the first and turned to his computer. Hunter Security had several databases they could check, plus they were signed up with several national companies that did background screening. He'd run these three through all the steps to see if he needed to alert Erikson.

The background check showed the name, any alias's, current address with the names of all people living at that address, and phone number along with a picture. It also showed any licenses held by the person being checked, any offences charged and if so, the disposition of the charge. Their financial status, any record of military service and any current liens or charges was also on the report.

All employees at Erikson International had to be fingerprinted, and the prints were checked against the IAFIS, or the Integrated Automated Fingerprint Identification System at the F.B.I headquarters. Due to the nature of the business, screening of employees was a major concern of Erikson International. Their records were in very good shape, probably one of the best that Jeff had ever run across.

He made a note of all the background searches he had made. He kept the three that he wanted to check further and put the rest back in the folder. Marty would notify Erikson of their findings. Jeff planned to have the last three checked before he left for the day.

It had been a busy day. Jeff decided he'd take a coffee break, then come back to finish checking the records from Erikson. He thought he'd check with MJ and see if she wanted to walk down to Tally's bar and grill for a cup.

When he got to MJ's office, she was gone. Jeff thought she probably was meeting with Roger and Kelly to go over their bodyguard duties. He decided to head on over by himself.

"I'm going over to Tally's for a cup." Jeff leaned over the counter by Marty's desk. "Get you anything?"

"I'm good," Marty replied, holding up her own cup. "I'm drinking the office swill."

Jeff grinned and waved and walked out. The sun was shining brightly on this cool October afternoon. The leaves were all turning and it was a beautiful afternoon.

He walked the short distance to Tally's and entered the side door.

"Hey Austin, how about a cup of your coffee?" Austin was standing behind the bar, watching a soccer game on TV. The place was empty. Austin turned, waved and picked up the pot on the back of the bar. He grabbed a cup and placed it on the bar in front of Jeff. "Whazzup Jeff?" he said, as he poured a cup of the aromatic coffee.

"Busy day Austin. Lot's going on. I needed a break." Jeff took a sip of the coffee. "Perfect!"

He and Austin watched the action on the TV and exchanged small talk. Jeff checked his watch and left money on the bar for the coffee. He waved at Austin and went back out the door he had come in. Austin returned to watching the soccer game.

When Jeff walked in the office, he stopped by Marty's desk. "MJ go out?"

"Yeah, she was meeting Kelly and Roger this afternoon. She said to tell you she was going to the gym to work out before she came home. Said she'd meet you there."

Jeff nodded and waved and walked back to his office. He hung his jacket up again and sat at the desk. He pulled the three folders of the employees from Erikson and logged back into his computer. For the next two hours, he ran background checks in depth on all three. Nothing bad showed up, but he still had a funny feeling about all three. They were almost too clean. Strange.

Chapter 6

MJ had briefed Roger and Kelly on the security required for Rebel Yell. It was something they were very familiar with, so the briefing didn't take much time. After exchanging their good-bye's, they all went their separate ways. MJ would meet them again when they picked up the Rebel Yell entourage at the airport. She was headed to the gym now for her workout.

She drove to the gym with the window down on the driver's side. She enjoyed the cool air blowing through her hair as she drove the quiet street towards the gym. The trees were all red and gold down this street. Leaves were falling, spiraling down into piles on the yards and sidewalks. This was her favorite time of the year. She parked in the customer lot by the gym. She and Jeff had a membership here and used it a lot.

She grabbed her gym bag from the back seat and entered the main lobby of the gym. She waved at Carol behind the desk and headed to the locker rooms. She did a quick change into her workout clothes and went out to the gym. She'd do a few laps around the workout floor to warm up. She noticed a few others doing the same thing. Her routine consisted of the warm-up laps, then some Tai Chi to stretch and loosen up. She skipped rope, and then she'd do some workout with the heavy bag, practicing her jumping kicks and chops with the side of her elbow. She practiced her jumping kick with a bag, and did exercises to strengthen her arms and neck muscles. A normal workout took between two and three hours.

She cut it short today after two hours and headed into the showers. The gym was nearly empty at this time of the day; it would get busy a little later in the afternoon. As she left the gym, she noticed a big dark man loitering by the entrance. He was wearing a black hoodie with the hood pulled over his face. He wore jeans and black sneakers. She got a feeling that he had been waiting for her. She kept track of him out of the corner of her eye as she headed to her car. There was another stranger dressed similarly standing by a car close to hers. All of her senses were on full alarm by now. She shifted her gym bag to her left hand and held the car keys in her right. The ignition key was locked between her first two fingers and she closed the fingers around the keys into a fist.

She had spent fifteen years as a field agent for the F.B.I. She was no stranger to street violence. She had been an instructor in self defense tactics at Quantico for a time, teaching other agents how to react in just such a situation as this. She knew instinctively they were going to attack. The best defense is offense. She slowed her approach to the car, letting the big man behind her come closer. As he got closer, the other man started towards her, his hand in the pocket of his hoodie. Not a good sign!

MJ pivoted on her left foot and brought her right foot in a swinging kick at the knee of the man behind her. She connected with the side of his leg, right at the knee joint. It was like hitting a tree, but his knee buckled, and he let out a yell and dropped to the ground. MJ continued swinging around, pivoting on her right foot and catching the man in front of her in the crotch. His eyes and mouth both gaped open and he let out a loud hiss as he dropped to his knees.

MJ dashed around the car, hitting the door locks on the remote. She grabbed the passenger door and opened it as she dropped her gym bag on the ground. Her Glock was locked in the glove compartment. As she struggled to get it unlocked, the two men staggered to a car and dropped into the front seat. As MJ got the glove box open, they peeled out of the parking lot, narrowly missing a post office van and took off down the street at high speed.

MJ managed to get the first two digits of the license before they got out of sight. The plates had been smeared with mud, but she imagined it was stolen anyway. She had her cell phone out and had speed dialed 911. She could hear the car in the distance, still speeding away as the dispatcher answered her call.

Chapter 7

Bobby Cantor finished installing Norton Ghost on the new laptop. He had all the systems backed up to external hard drives that he kept locked up in the basement of his house. It was dark outside; everybody else had gone home, except for the two guys in the back room monitoring the central station. The central station was manned 24/7 with rotating shifts. He looked at his watch, almost nine o'clock. Bobby enjoyed his work so much he lost track of time. Jeff and MJ let him work whatever hours he wanted. He was compensated well enough and he liked everybody here.

Bobby locked the laptop in the computer cabinet drawer of his shop. He had built the cabinet himself to hold the laptops and extra software and disks. The drawers and the cabinet were lined to prevent unwanted electromagnetic fields from erasing any data from the laptops or the software itself. He took his coffee cup over to the sink and rinsed it out and put it on the sideboard. He walked out of the shop, turning off the lights as he left. He had a program on the SiFi channel that he had recorded to his Tivo that he wanted to watch tonight.

He went by the monitoring room and waved good night to the two guys in the central station. They waved their good nights as he left the office and locked the door behind him.

As he walked towards his van, he noticed two men walking towards him from across the parking. He noticed them because both were walking a little funny, one was limping badly and the other was walking lightly, as if his feet were sore. They looked ominous in their hoodies and dark clothes. Bobby fingered the stun gun in his jacket pocket. He flipped the switch on the side, just in case.

As he neared the van, they approached him. Sore foot was closer; the limper was in front of the van. Bobby had parked facing the parking lot, so he didn't have to back up to leave. There weren't any cars on either side of the van. Bobby had his keys in his left hand and the Stun Master in his right. The Stun Master was designed to look like a cell phone. Unless you looked closely, you couldn't tell it wasn't.

He didn't like the look he was getting from Sore Foot. The man had his right hand in his hoodie pocket and he reached for Bobby with his left.

Bobby stepped closer and pressed the Stun Master to Sore Foots chest. He pressed the trigger, sending a 600,000 volt jolt to his attacker. Sore Foot jerked spasmodically, then dropped, sitting on his rear. He had dropped a short piece of pipe when he jerked his hand out of his pocket. He would be out of commission for about three minutes, until the effects of the stun gun wore off.

Bobby looked at Limper. Limper had rushed over when Sore Foot went down. He rushed a little too quickly and tripped over Sore Foot. He grabbed at Bobby as he went down, pushing Bobby up against the van. Bobby leaned over and gave him a shot with the stun gun too. Now both men were twitching in the parking lot in front of the van.

Usually at this time of night, there was at least a little foot traffic around. Tonight, there was none except for a couple out by the street. They were deep in discussion and didn't notice the commotion in the parking lot.

Bobby didn't wait. He ran back to the office, unlocked the door and hurried back to the monitoring room.

"Hey Jack, I just got attacked in the parking lot. Call 911 and come out here to help me hold these guys. You too Ernie." Bobby turned and headed back towards the parking lot with Jack and Ernie following at a run.

As they exited the office, they saw the two men, running towards a car parked by the street. They were hobbling and helping each other stand up, not moving too fast. Bobby and his friends started after them when the bigger of the two, turned and pulled a gun from his waistband. He fired off two shots at the trio.

All three hit the ground. Bobby heard glass breaking behind him. He squirmed around to see Jack and Ernie on the ground also. They appeared to be alright, their eyes were probably as big as his own.

Bobby heard a car start, then peel off down the street. It was too dark to get a good description. All three of them gained their feet and looked at each other.

"You O.K., Bobby?" Ernie asked. "How about you, Jack?"

Jack and Bobby responded simultaneously, "yeah, yeah, fine."

"Back to the office, we gotta call 9-1-1." Bobby started running back to the office. The couple that had been walking down the street was cautiously heading their way. "What's going on?" the man shouted.

"Muggers!" shouted Bobby, motioning them towards the office. "We're going to call the cops."

All five of them huddled inside the office. Bobby went to the phone on Marty's desk and dialed, Jack headed back to the central station to see if any of the video cameras had recorded the attack. Ernie sat in one of the chairs, motioning to the couple to join him.

Bobby finished his call to the police and then called Jeff's cell phone.

"Jeff! Jack and Ernie and I just got shot at by some dudes here at the office. The cops are on the way, and they took off." Bobby was talking fast and his hands were still shaking from the encounter. He stopped to listen, his eyes getting bigger. "Is she alright?" He nodded and nodded, then hung up the phone after a mumbled "good-bye".

Bobby turned to Ernie and the couple; all sitting together, the man and women were holding hands, visibly shaken by the ordeal. "MJ got attacked earlier tonight. She and Jeff are at the police station now."

"Holy cow!" Ernie sat up straight. "She O.K.?"

"Yeah, sounds like maybe the same two guys. She did a number on both of them, but they got away."

Ernie grinned. "Bet she did! They got off lucky!"

The couple looked between Bobby and Ernie, "What is going on?"

"We don't know, but we need you to stick around for a little bit. Cops are on the way and will take statements. You'll be able to leave soon." Bobby got up and walked over to the coffee pot. "Anybody else want some coffee?"

Chapter 8

It was early the next morning by the time all the statements had been taken, complaints filed and everyone had left. Jeff and MJ were alone in Jeff's office. Jack and Ernie had finished their shift and been replaced by Alice and Foster. It was finally quiet. MJ and Jeff were slumped in their chairs. They had bounced ideas off of each other for the last hour, but had resolved nothing. They couldn't figure out why the attacks.

"I'm beat." Jeff looked over at MJ, "You look beat too, and you should be, you've had a very busy day!"

MJ yawned in agreement. "Wonder who those assholes were? I wish I could have gotten in a few more licks." She smiled in thought, "I bet they were surprised when Bobby zapped them. Wish I could have seen that. Talk about a rough day, those two ought to be looking at a new line of work."

"Ha!" Jeff barked, "When they heal up, I wouldn't be surprised if they do." He reached over and squeezed MJ's arm. "Let's hang it up kiddo, we aren't getting anywhere."

They stopped by the central station to say good night to Alice and Foster. In the parking, they looked around nervously, but no one was around. They got into their separate cars and left, MJ taking the lead, Jeff close behind.

At Jeff's house, they parked their cars in the garage. The external and internal lights came on automatically from the motion sensors. The door from the garage to the house had a keypad and a biometric fingerprint pad next to it. Jeff entered the code and placed his index finger on the pad. An audible click told them the locks were de-activated. Jeff opened the door and led MJ inside. They walked into the master bedroom and disrobed, dressing in their pajamas without the usual banter. Exhaustion had taken its toll.

Both were asleep shortly after crawling under the blankets.

Chapter 9

Jeff awoke to the exploring fingers of MJ. The sun was shining through the blinds of the bedroom. Jeff did a little exploring of his own and he and MJ wound up tangled in the sheets. After, they lay there, breathing heavy and holding one another.

Finally, it was MJ that broke loose and jumped out of bed. "Shower time!" Jeff rolled out and followed her into the shower.

Finally, they were both seated at the dinette drinking coffee. "Look at the time! We need to get to the office and see if anybody has found out what prompted the attacks yesterday." Jeff dumped the remains of his third cup of coffee into the sink. He grabbed his trusty jacket from the back of the chair and picked his cell phone up out of the charger. MJ was ahead of him, swinging her purse over her arm.

MJ left the garage first, Jeff right behind her. They drove in tandem to the office, both watching carefully around them as they drove. They arrived without incident and walked in together.

Marty was at the desk, looking warily at them. "What in the hell is going on?"

MJ turned her palms up and shrugged. "Who the hell knows?" She smiled at Marty and patted her on the shoulder. "We're going to try and find out, that's for sure."

Jeff was right behind her. "Have you heard anything from Captain Harris or the PD?" He leaned on the counter.

"I got a call first thing. Captain Harris would like to see you two at the station. I tried to find out if they had anything new, but he just said he'd bring you up to date when you got together." Jeff could tell it was really bugging Marty, not being in the loop. He took a few minutes to bring her up to speed. By the time he finished, Marty's mouth was hanging open.

"Good god Gerty!" Marty shook her head. "I wonder what in the hell brought all that on."

"Wish we knew. I hope Harris has something for us." Jeff headed back to his office. "Have you seen Bobby yet?"

"He called, said he'd be in later. He didn't tell me anything, the rat." Marty looked after Bobby like he was her own son. She knew he didn't want her to worry.

Jeff knew how she felt. "Bobby can take care of himself. He gave those two something to think about, that's for sure." Marty had to grin at that. "Wish I'd seen that, or no, maybe I don't. I probably would have had a heart attack." The phone rang, and she turned to answer it. Jeff went on to his office.

Chapter 10

MJ and Jeff drove to the police station in Jeff's car. They parked in the visitors spot and walked in the lobby of the building. Getting to Captain Harris's office required going through the metal detector and getting a visitors badge. Captain Harris had already cleared them, so it was a quick process. They took the familiar walk to the Captains office and knocked on the door. Harris's voice boomed at them, "Come in." He was sitting at his desk with the phone to his ear. "Yes sir, I understand sir, they're here now." He hung up the phone and grimaced at Jeff and MJ. "What a mess." He stood and shook hands with the two of them, waving them to the chairs in front of his desk. "The media was informed about your mishaps yesterday; they'll be heading after you next. That was the Chief on the phone, he's asking for your help to get this resolved."

"Sure John, anything we can do. We want this resolved as much as you do." Jeff leaned forward, his elbows on his knees. MJ just sat quietly, her experience with the F.B.I. taking over.

There was a book on the captain's desk. They knew without asking that it was mug shots. Harris turned it so it was facing them. "Might as well take a look. We picked out as many as we could from MJ's and the other witnesses descriptions. If we get lucky, we'll find those two and get them talking."

Jeff pushed the book to MJ; he hadn't seen either of the men. "I suppose Bobby is coming in for a look too?"

"Yes, he called earlier; he's on his way down now." Harris turned to MJ. "Glad we've got an experienced and trained observer to take a look. You can be a big help." MJ looked up at him and smiled, then went back to perusing the book. She was concentrating on each picture.

Harris and Jeff talked softly to each other while MJ went through the pictures. Harris kept glancing hopefully at MJ, waiting for her to find what they all wanted.

Suddenly, MJ slapped the page she was looking at. "Here's one of them!" She had her finger on the picture of an ugly looking man with some numbers at the bottom of the page. It was obviously a booking photo. "Get this sucker and we'll find his partner." MJ had a triumphant look on her face. It was mirrored by Harris. "Keep looking, the partner might be in there too." Harris was scribbling notes on a pad as he got the information from the picture MJ had singled out. MJ took the book back and started looking again as Harris turned to his computer and started tapping on the keyboard.

Flipping through the pages, MJ stopped again, slapping another picture. "Here he is!" She kept her finger on the picture and turned the book so Harris could see the one she had picked out. "Partner in crime!" MJ pumped her fist in the air. "GOTCHA!"

Harris was grinning ear to ear as he pounded the keyboard. He paused and hit the print key. The printer beside his desk whirred into life and started spitting out paper. Harris grabbed the sheets as they came out. He started reading the first page. He whistled. "Whew! Quite a pedigree. Assault, armed robbery, burglary. His rap sheet goes back a long ways. Bet he has a juvie sheet too." Harris turned to the next batch of papers. "His partner is right up there too. More of the same, both of them have served time in the state pen, no federal charges."

"There will be now," MJ said, "attempted kidnapping will work. I can get my old buddies from the bureau to jump on this too."

Harris wasn't that enthusiastic about getting the feds involved, but he wasn't going to quibble.

"Let's see what we can find out about their present whereabouts." He turned back to the computer, tapping on the keys again. "They're not on parole, they've served their time for the charges, must have had a good mouthpiece, they got reduced sentences in a plea bargain." He hit the print key again and the printer started spitting out more paper.

"We've got their last known addresses. Guess what, they live in the same apartment complex." Harris was grinning again. He reached for the phone and started barking orders into it. "Bring these goons in for questioning, and be careful, they may be armed and dangerous." He turned back to Jeff and MJ. "Better safe than sorry." He handed over the printouts with the pictures and information on the two suspects. The big guy was named Harry Longstreet, aka Harry Long, Harry Street, and 'Longdrink'. His buddy was Ansel

Worthington, aka Andy Worth, and 'Anshole'. "Apt names," Jeff thought. He handed the sheets to MJ.

"Bobby will probably confirm these two. From his description, they have to be the same guys that attacked MJ." Harris chuckled, "After MJ finished with them, it made them easier to identify, what with the body damages."

MJ looked up and grinned. "My pleasure. Wish I could have given them some more identifying characteristics, like broken limbs, contusions, you know, that kind of thing."

"It's almost funny, "Harris said, "Two hard-cases like this thought they had easy pickings with a cute little gal and a geek. Just goes to show you, don't underestimate the opposition."

Chapter 11

Just before they left the police station, Bobby Cantor showed up and identified the two that attacked MJ were the same two that came after him. Captain Harris complimented Bobby on his actions. Bobby was a little flustered from all of the attention. He was a bright red, even though he was grinning ear to ear.

Back at the office, Marty caused Bobby even more embarrassment by giving him a big hug in front of Jeff and MJ. Bobby escaped back to his shop while MJ and Jeff met in her office with Marty. "We have to all be on our toes until we can figure out what's behind these attacks" MJ was looking at Marty. "Marty, you are our front line of defense. Make sure you have pepper spray handy and check the panic button today to make sure it's functioning properly."

"You sound like an agent again, MJ." Marty gave them both a wave. "I'll go check the button right now and make sure I have enough spray." She headed back to her desk at the front office.

MJ and Jeff went over the schedule for the day. MJ would be meeting with Roger and Kelly at the airport.

Roger and Kelly would escort Rebel Yell to the hotel and MJ would meet once more with the agent, Krug, to finalize the contract.

Jeff planned on going to Erikson International to meet with the head of security there and go through instructions on the access control with him. He was going to stop by the PD to meet with Harris to review some of the other break-ins that had been going on. Harris was assembling a team to investigate the break-ins and had asked Jeff to give them some pointers on what to look for. Jeff had assembled some hand-outs to give to the members of the team.

"I'm going to whip up a PowerPoint presentation to give to Harris and his team." Jeff said, sitting at his desk, "You meeting with the guys at the airport or here?"

"At the airport," MJ looked at her watch, "and I'd better get moving." She picked up her purse and gave Jeff a quick kiss before heading out the door.

"Be careful!" Jeff shouted after her. She was already gone.

Jeff fired up his PowerPoint program and started working on his presentation. He modified an existing program and saved it as a PowerPoint show on his thumb drive. He ejected the drive and stuck in his shirt pocket. Taking his jacket from the rack, he headed out the door. He waved at Marty on the way out and got in his car and headed for Erikson's.

Chapter 12

Erikson's head of security was a man named Jim
Saunders. Jim was a retired administrator from the
state's department of public safety. He had experience
as a patrol officer and as a department head. A really
good man to have running this show. Jeff had heard of
him, but they had never met. After the introductions,
they found they had a lot of common acquaintances,
mostly from the law enforcement community.

Jeff did a quick outline of how the access control
system worked. Anyone that wanted to enter the main
facility, other than the offices, was required to go
through a man trap entrance gate that was equipped
with metal detectors. All bags were searched and x-
rayed. All doors in the storage area were kept locked
and alarmed. The locks were the magnetic type that had
a battery back-up. The doors were steel with just a small
access window of reinforced bullet proof glass. The
windows were small, and were there for viewing
purposes mainly. There was a closed circuit video
system that covered all entrances, the parking, and the
grounds around the facility. The cameras were equipped
with night vision, pan and tilt and zoom capabilities. The

control center recorded all of the cameras, 24/7 and each camera had its own monitor. A video switcher allowed the control center operator to switch any camera to the large flat screen for more detailed viewing. Each camera was equipped with a speaker that allowed the operator to communicate with anyone in the viewing area. Ultra sensitive microphones on each camera allowed listen in capability. The microphones were controlled by the operator. The recording was all done in a multiplexed mode. That way, each camera could be called up individually to review what was recorded.

Multiplex was a technique where up to 16 cameras were recorded, one frame at a time, and then saved. In playback mode, any individual camera could be called up for viewing with a nearly real time. It saved time and space on the disk to which the cameras were recorded.

Restricted areas were kept locked and access was only provided to personnel that had been cleared for access. A keypad and a biometric fingerprint pad were both connected to the locking mechanism on the door.

Three attempts were the maximum allowed. After that, an alarm was sounded at the control center.

The control center was manned around the clock by specially trained personnel. Access to the control panel was controlled also. Each controller checked in with the dispatcher at the sheriff's office hourly. If a call was not received, a car was dispatched to contact the facility.

Jeff explained the function of all the equipment as he and Saunders made the tour of the facility and the control room.

"Your building has its own power generator. In case of an outage, the generator kicks in. The system is what is known as a UPS, or uninterruptible power supply. Deep discharge marine batteries supply power until the diesel powered generator kicks in." Jeff and Saunders were in the utility room of the building. The utility room was also part of the security system. There were cameras mounted at strategic points around the room. "All the halls and doors have their own emergency lights, and the computer system has its own UPS." Jeff pointed out the various switchboxes and equipment. "I've left a recommended schedule for testing all the equipment.

All the smoke detectors, heat sensors and other emergency detection equipment have their own schedule for testing."

Saunders nodded his approval. "Looks like you've covered everything. This place is probably as safe as Fort Knox." They both laughed, "Better safe than sorry." Jeff said, that comment being his mantra.

Saunders led the way back to his office. Jeff observed the areas as he passed through them. Everything looked exactly as he wanted them. Security should be top notch in this facility.

They had coffee in Saunders office. Jim Saunders sat in his chair behind his desk, Jeff in front of him. They reviewed what they had just observed in the tour.

"God damn! It looks good." Saunders said, smiling at Jeff.

"I agree. It's like a dream come true. It's as good as it gets." Jeff leaned back in his chair. The coffee was excellent and he felt really good about the run through the plant. Considering the inventory that Erikson carried, nothing else would suffice. It would have been a nightmare if a break-in occurred there.

Jeff and Saunders clicked their coffee cups in a toast. "Here's to tight security!"

Chapter 13

Jeff left the Erikson compound with a good feeling. This is the way it should be done. Leave nothing to chance, cover all the possibilities. His only concern was that he didn't have control over whom the company employed for their security team. As far as the physical security, there wasn't much more that could be done. The place was like a fortress.

Jeff was reviewing the tour as he headed down to the PD for his meeting with Harris. He kept thinking about the weird attacks that had happened to MJ and Bobby. He couldn't figure out what had motivated them. It was unnerving. Had it been kidnapping behind the attacks? If so, why? What would have been the kidnappers' demands? He couldn't come up with anything. It was a mystery.

Jeff was still amazed that MJ had chosen him. He was nearly in awe of her. She was drop dead gorgeous, smarter than him, and knew her business. He considered himself the luckiest man on the planet. He wanted to spend every minute of every day with her, and had to restrain himself from being obviously obsessive. MJ just took it all with a smile.

It was another great day; sun was shining, temps in the mid seventies. Jeff rolled down his window and took it all in. As he looked around, smiling at everything, he noticed a black SUV in his rear view mirror. He lost his smile. He had noticed a black SUV as he left Eriksons. Traffic was light, so Jeff decided to take a few turns to see what the SUV did. He took a right at the next corner, turning on a red light as there was no oncoming traffic. No SUV. He was getting paranoid. He smiled again, and made two lefts to head back towards the PD. He had no sooner got back on the main road when he noticed the SUV was behind him again, about four car lengths back. It was a Cadillac Escalade. He sped up and the Caddy kept the same distance behind him. He slowed down, it did likewise. He picked up his cell and hit the speed dial for Harris' direct number.

Harris picked up on the first ring. "Captain Harris."

"John, it's Jeff. I'm on Prospect drive, heading for your office. I'm being followed by a black Escalade."

Harris didn't question what made Jeff think he was being followed. "What's your 20?" Harris used the ten code abbreviation for location.

"Just passed Evergreen gardens" Evergreen was a big cemetery on the city outskirts.

"Stay on Prospect; I'll have some cars pick you up. We'll see what they're up to."

Jeff flipped the phone closed and laid it on the passenger seat. He glanced up at the mirror, the car was still there.

He was on a deserted stretch of road. No houses, just a few drives that headed off of the highway on both sides. No cars in sight in either direction. He glanced up again and saw that the Escalade had sped up and was approaching from behind at a high rate of speed. It pulled out to pass. Jeff watched as it pulled alongside of him. The rear window slid down and a hand came out with something in it.

What the hell? Jeff thought, it looked like a small rock. The arm threw the rock out in front of Jeff as they sped by, picking up more speed as it left his hand.

Grenade! Jeff hit the brakes and yanked hard on the wheel. He went off the road on the opposite side, bouncing and jarring as he slid sideways through the grass.

He heard the explosion and felt the concussion as fragments peppered the side of his car. He had his hands full just keeping control as he slowed to a stop at the edge of a driveway. Luckily, there hadn't been a drainage ditch along this stretch of road or he would most likely have flipped the car. He finally got the car stopped and just sat there for a few minutes, hands still white knuckled on the wheel.

He looked for his cell. It had slid off of the seat and was out of sight. He checked for the Escalade, but there was no sign of it anywhere. He got out of the car and went around to the passenger side. The side of the KIA was peppered with small holes and dents from the grenade fragments. He checked the area. Everybody must have been at work; there was no sign of life. Opening the passenger door, he found his cell wedged between the seat and the floor on the door side. He flipped it open. It still worked.

He hit the call button to connect to Harris again; he would know the deal and have the troops on the lookout already.

Again, he answered on the first ring. "Captain Harris."

"Me again John, they tossed a grenade at me. Have your guys be aware. I'm o.k., just a little damage to the car. They didn't stop after they tossed me the pineapple, no sign of them around anywhere."

"Jesus Jeff! What the hell is going on? Did you get a plate by any chance?"

"Wish I knew. Must have pissed off somebody. No plate, just that it's a black Caddy Escalade, new one. You'd think it would be pretty easy to spot."

"Maybe not, when I called it in, dispatch told me they just had one reported stolen."

"Great, they've probably dumped it by now." Jeff looked down the road and saw a patrol car headed his way, lights flashing. "I see one of your guys coming now. I'll call you back in a short."

Jeff closed the phone and walked to the front of his car, waiting for the black and white to pull up. The car stopped and Jeff could see the officer talking into his microphone. He put the mike back on the clip and exited the car. It was an old friend of Jeff's, Tom Wilkins. "Hey Tom, having some problems here."

"I guess!" Tom adjusted his utility belt, then stuck out his hand. They shook hands and Tom walked over to look at Jeff's car. He whistled. "Man, these dudes are serious. A grenade?"

"Yep, you can see there on the road where it went off. Didn't do too much damage, luckily, there weren't any other cars around. It could have been messy."

Tom was running his hands over the punctures in the side of Jeff's car. "Damn! You know this KIA has side air bags. That's what stopped most of the shrapnel from getting in and doing a number on you."

"Wondered why I didn't get hit. Guess I'll need to get them replaced too."

"Better to replace the airbags than your hide." Tom took the mike from his portable from its holder on his shoulder. "Unit 225 will be 10-7 at this 20. Notify the Captain." He listened to the radio, Jeff couldn't make out what was said, and then Tom keyed his mike again. "That's a 10-4."

They stood by Jeff's car as Jeff filled Tom in on his episode and told him about MJ's and Bobby's encounters the night before.

Another patrol car appeared in the distance. They waited for it to pull in behind Tom's car. More talk on the radio and the next officer joined them. Jeff didn't know him, but Tom introduced them. The new officers' name was Randy.

"No sign of the Escalade anywhere. I wanted to check in with you here before I put the news out on the radio, just in case. Never know who all is listening in anymore."

Tom and Jeff agreed. Jeff spoke up, "They've probably dumped it. I talked to Harris; he told me that one had been reported stolen."

"Easy to do along this stretch of highway, lot's of drives and county roads." Randy pointed to the drives on either side of the road.

They discussed the incident some more, then Tom filled out an accident report. He handed it to Jeff. "You'll probably need this for the insurance company." Jeff took the form and folded it into his jacket pocket.

"Thanks Tom. You guys keep your eyes open. Those people are serious. I'm heading in for a meet with Harris. Thanks for coming out." They checked to make sure Jeff's car would run alright, then called in for a crew to come out and sweep the area for any evidence, although they all agreed that chances of finding anything of importance were slim.

Tom and Randy waved and got into their respective vehicles. They turned around on the highway, and headed back towards town. Jeff followed, keeping them in sight until he got to the city limits. He turned off to head to police headquarters. He made a call to MJ. She wanted to come see him right away, but he calmed her down and told her they'd be in touch later. He still had his meeting with Captain Harris about the attacks of the previous day. Now, he had more to discuss.

Chapter 14

Harris greeted Jeff at his office. After expressing his concerns over the latest attack, he and Jeff sat at his desk, both with coffees in front of them.

"This has to be related to Hunter Security." Harris sat his cup back on his desk and leaned forward towards Jeff. "Something you have started or some new client must have triggered something."

"I think so too." Jeff sat his cup back carefully; his hands still had a little tremor from the adrenaline kick from his attack. "We just picked up the security for Erikson International. As you know, they deal in all kinds of weapons. They would be the obvious target. We also have the protection contract for Rebel Yell, the musicians. We're, or at least MJ and crew are doing the escort service. I can't see any real problem there."

"I tend to agree." Harris shuffled the reports on his desk. "The attack on you and Bobby would seem to rule out the musicians. It appears they're trying to disrupt your central station activities, or divert your focus to protecting yourselves."

"Has to be," Jeff said. "We do the monitoring for Eriksons. But even if they could stop the monitoring, they still have the security personnel on sight, and, the sheriff patrols."

"I haven't seen the setup at the plant, but knowing you, I bet it's pretty secure."

"You should go out and take a look. It would give you an idea of just how secure it is, plus, you might spot something that I've missed. Another pair of eyes is always good." Jeff opened his briefcase and laid a folder on Harris's desk. "Here's the overall plan."

Harris opened the folder and slowly went over each plan and diagram. He pointed out some of the features for Jeff to explain and examined each diagram.

"Damn! Looks tight." Harris sat back and looked over at Jeff. "Only way for someone to break in would be by helicopter." He tapped the photo of the plant. "Even then, it would take a good sized crew to carry it off."

"I had considered that in the initial plan. Erikson put the kibosh on that, too expensive."

"How would you even manage to do that?" Harris rubbed his hand on his bald head.

Jeff smiled at the gesture. "Sensors, cameras, traps. Erikson was concerned because they have their own helicopter to commute to the airport. He was afraid it might get caught in the traps, or trigger false alarms. It was a valid concern, even though I explained that it would just protect the rooftop. Their helipad is out front, by their parking lot." Jeff pointed out the areas concerned on the map of the area.

"Probably excessive. It would have added quite a bit of extra expense, I just wanted him to have the option." Jeff took the folder back as Harris handed it over. "I'm really more concerned that I didn't get to do the actual security team. Erikson hired their own, some of them from their own employees. I would rather have had a professional service, although I have to admit, he's got some very good people at the top."

"Yes, I remember Jim Saunders from the old days. Good man knows his stuff. He was a good administrator too." Harris pulled his rolodex over. "I'll give Jim a call; see if he can arrange a tour for me and a couple of my guys. I don't have a number for him, you have one?"

Jeff handed over one of the cards he had picked up from Erikson. "Here's their main number, you can get Saunders through there. I've got his direct number too." He fished out his cell and punched a few keys. He handed the cell to Harris. "That's Saunders direct line."

Harris wrote down the number on the card from Erikson and handed the cell back to Jeff. He stuck the card in the corner of his desk blotter and looked back up at Jeff.

"Had another burglary early this morning. Same M.O. as before must have used that cell jammer thing again too. These guys are getting bolder." Harris did the head rub again. "I've got a regular crime wave on my hands, what with all these burglaries and the attacks on you guys."

"Wish I could do more to help John, but my priorities right now are watching out for my own people."

Jeff stood up to leave. He put the folder back in his briefcase and closed it up. He stuck his hand out to John Harris.

Harris took his hand and gave it a firm shake. "You watch out on your end Jeff. We're going to put extra patrol around your place, and I'm going to give the Sheriff a call and give him a heads up too. You let me know if we can do anything else. We've got two detectives working on your case now. Let's hope they can come up with something."

"I hope they can find those two goons that attacked MJ and Bobby. I'd like to have some time with them myself."

Harris nodded, "Know what you mean, wouldn't mind that either, but I'll be happy just to get them off the street."

Chapter 15

Back at the office, Jeff had Bobby and Marty meet by Marty's desk. She still had to run the office and watch the phones. Jeff had ideas for both of them. He filled them in on the latest attack on him, and his discussions with Captain Harris.

"So far, we've been lucky." Jeff started. "I think we really need to be on our toes here. Marty, I don't like the idea of you being out front here all by yourself. You're too exposed for one thing, and if they decide to hit here, you'd be the first target."

Marty shifted uncomfortably in her chair. "What do you want me to do? Shoot first?"

Jeff smiled at her enthusiasm, it sounded like she liked the idea. "Not really, not that I don't think you could do it, I just don't want to put you in that position." Marty shifted in her chair again.

"I think we need a buffer zone. Let's move you back to my office. We'll move your file cabinets and the copy machine back there. We can connect the fax machine back there too. We'll just switch users on the computer. I'll use the one up here, you can use mine."

Bobby spoke up. "I'm in the process of backing everything up. It might be a good idea to remote our monitoring too." He looked from Jeff to Marty, "I like the idea of getting Marty away from the front, but it won't be much safer for you to be there either."

Jeff agreed, "You're right, of course, but I'm out of the office most of the time. We can put a temporary waiting room right here by the front door, have a free standing wall with a door installed. You can connect a video camera and intercom here couldn't you Bobby?"

"Sure, no problem, but will that stop anybody that really wants in?"

"I think I'll get Roger and Kelly to work shifts here in the front too. They're both trained as security officers, and they have permits to carry. They won't be available until after the concert, but it will take a day or two to get everything set up anyway. The concert is tomorrow night and Saturday night. If we can get the office changed over this week-end, we should be ready by Monday morning."

Marty and Bobby exchanged a look. Marty spoke first. "It will be different, but it works for me if it works for you."

"I'd feel better if we did it." Bobby said. "I'll be happy to work through the week-end."

"Me too," Marty chimed in, "I don't have any big plans."

Jeff looked at the two of them. They were like two kids planning a sleep over. "Overtime for everybody."

Marty and Bobby did a high five. "Whoopee!"

"I'll touch base with MJ and we'll make plans. Bobby, you can start on this project now. Let's put off the backups 'til we get this done."

"I'm on it boss." Bobby stood up and headed back to his shop. Marty went to her desk and started stacking files. Jeff headed to his office. He had some packing to do.

Chapter 16

Jeff called MJ on her cell. She was at the airport. Rebel Yell was due to land any minute. Jeff ran his ideas past her. She was still upset from the attack on him earlier and she agreed to the plan immediately. She promised to ask Roger and Kelly and get back to him. They would meet after she got the escort started. Roger and Kelly would handle it from then on.

Jeff got his files that he would need for the next few days and put them in a box. Bobby would move the phones as Marty had the master console with all the extensions on it. Bobby knew how to switch the lines at the demark point in the office. He'd take care of that and the rest of the technical work.

Two hours later, Jeff had switched offices with Marty. He had relocated the desk to give him less exposure to the outside. They didn't get much walk-in business anyway, mostly deliveries. He felt even better when he had his 1911 Colt fastened under the desk for a quick draw. He had a taser and some pepper spray handy too, just in case. Marty was feisty enough, but she didn't have the training that the rest of them had. If anything happened to her, Jeff would never forgive himself.

Jeff figured by the time they got the rest of the set up done, they should be pretty safe for now. He wished Captain John would catch those two goons. Maybe he could make them talk and find out what this was all about.

Chapter 17

Jeff reviewed the reports he had received from Captain Harris. He noticed that all of the successful burglaries had taken place at businesses that were covered by other security systems and companies. None of Hunter Security clients had been hit successfully. In each case, the police had arrived on the scene of the Hunter sites before the premises had been compromised. The number of attempts was staggering. Sometimes there had been several attacks in one night. It appeared the burglars would make the initial attempt, then wait for a response. If none came, they completed their break-in. If the police arrived, they moved on to the next target.

Jeff made note of each successful attempt and which company did the monitoring of their security. He couldn't figure out why his company was the only one that had been able to thwart the crooks. He wrote the other companies names and numbers down in a list and started calling.

The first company on the list was a local one. Like Jeff, they had come from the law-enforcement field and started business on their own. Three of their clients had been successfully burgled. He knew the owner of the business. He had over thirty years as a cop. He was street smart; he should have been able to apply his experienced to his new business.

Jeff decided to give him a call.

"Safe House Security." the voice on the other end said.

"This is Jeff Hunter, from Hunter Security. Is Bob Fleming in?" Bob was the owner of Safe House Security.

"One moment." There was a click followed by some typical music, then another click as a line was picked up.

"Hey Jeff, how're tricks?" Bob Fleming had attended several security expos with Jeff. They had even shared a room at one of the conventions in Las Vegas.

"Good Bob. I'll get right to the point, I've been working with Captain Harris, down at the PD, and I've got a list of all these burglaries that have been taking place."

"I've got that list too. Bad news for the industry. How in the hell have you been spared?" Fleming was asking in a joking tone, he sounded really interested in Jeff's response.

"That's what I want to find out." Jeff picked up the list, going down the different businesses that were covered by Fleming's company. "What are we doing different that has kept us off the hook?"

"I dunno, I thought we had all the top end included in our systems. We have entrance exit delays, video monitoring, we have telephone line monitors, and cell phone backups."

Jeff listened and thought what else they had that would have protected their companies that Fleming didn't have.

"Your telephone line monitors just sound a local audible, right?"

"Yeah, don't yours?"

"Yes, but I've noticed the local audibles have all been disabled, even on the attempts on our systems. They still gave up on ours, but not yours. It's got to be something else."

"We've discussed this before Jeff, when we were comparing our systems. A lot of our equipment is the same as yours. Only difference I see is that we have different central stations, but both of our central stations are local, run by our own people."

"I'm going to have to go over our systems to see what it could possibly be. I'm sure you've already pulled your curly blond locks out doing the same."

Fleming chuckled on his end. "Yeah, I'll be bald if this doesn't stop. My only consolation has been that there were other systems getting hit. You seem to be the only exception. I figured you had turned to the bad side and were pulling the jobs yourself. I thought about turning you in to Harris for the reward."

It was Jeff's turn to chuckle. "In your dreams. If I did it, I'd never get caught, and I'd never do it in my own back yard."

"Yep, that's what made me think it wasn't you. You're smarter than that."

"If I come up with anything, I'll be sure to let you know. I'm going to check out a couple of these other outfits and see if I can find out what it is."

They chatted a few more minutes, and then Jeff hung up. Fleming was a good friend and a sharp security man. Jeff decided to check their own procedures. Must be something he had overlooked.

He headed back to the central station. He entered his access card and used the pad to enter his fingerprint. The door opened, and Jeff walked into the cool dark room. Video monitors lined the walls. Receivers with onboard printers were clicking along. It was nearing closing time and the panels were receiving the closing reports from each business as they locked up for the night.

Everything was running according to plan. No alarms, no malfunctions. Everything was just as it should be. Jeff remembered the first few weeks running the businesses. There were alarms going off all the time. 99% were employee errors as people were exposed to new methods and new equipment. A lot of training in the field had finally reduced those errors to a minimum.

Jeff went to an empty terminal and sat at the desk. The two employees running the other terminals were too busy monitoring their own accounts to pay him much attention. They had waved at his entrance then returned to watching the screens in front of them.

Jeff punched in his code and brought up the history screen. He picked an account at random and went down the checklist. Openings and closings, employees logging in, computer terminals accessed, and the other normal activities that went on in a secured environment. He scrolled down the list. After the closing, things settled down. No transmissions except for the handshake connections.

That had to be it! He had forgotten about the handshakes. He was one of the few that insisted on a handshake connection on each alarm panel they installed. What it amounted to was a simple transmission from the customer panel to the central station showing that they were in contact with each other. It was just a simple call that went out every fifteen minutes. It just established that the panel was still in contact with the central station. If the handshake didn't complete, it activated another alarm at the central station that demanded that a physical check be made. The handshake could either be made from the landline, or in case of a failure, through the backup cell phone. As long as the handshake came through, no action was taken or needed. It just verified that communications were still intact.

Jeff was excited now. He'd have to check with the companies that had been hit and see if they used the backup handshake system. A lot of companies didn't because of the expense, and it required another degree of programming that wasn't available on all systems. It wasn't a practical addition where the call would generate an extra fee through the provider, whether it be a landline or cellular. The calls could be expensive. Jeff had decided to absorb the extra cost in exchange for the added security. Looks like it had paid off.

Maybe that explained the attacks on him and his employees. It might be organized crime outfits trying to do a big push on burglaries. If Hunter Security was the fly in the ointment, it made sense they'd try to shut them down. Jeff picked up the list of the other security companies and headed out to his desk.

The first call was to Fleming. He agreed with Jeff. The handshake was the only difference they could come up with that made sense. Fleming said he just might have to start incorporating it in his systems too. The rest of the calls seemed to confirm Jeff's conclusions. He was the only company that had the handshake, along with all the other backup options. For some of the security outfits, it still wasn't a viable option unless the customer would be willing to pick up the extra cost.

Jeff looked at the clock. Almost five o'clock. He knew Captain Harris didn't have regular hours but he decided to try him at the office anyway. After three rings, it went to the dispatchers' desk. Jeff told the dispatcher he'd try later. He dialed Harris's cell phone and the Captain picked up on the first ring.

"Harris." He sounded brusque and irritated.

"It's me John, Jeff Hunter. If you've got a minute, I think I've got another lead on the burglaries."

"Oh, hi Jeff, at least that's good news. I've got another mess on my hands now." Jeff could hear voices and sirens in the background.

"What's up Cap?"

"Those two thugs that attacked MJ and Bobby?" Harris was drowned out by noise and Jeff could hear him shouting to someone, but couldn't make out the words.

"You still there Jeff?"

"Yeah, I'm here, what's up?"

"We're in the process of bagging up their bodies. We pulled them out of the lake a few minutes ago. Gunshot to the head, assassin type."

"Jeez! I'll let you finish there. Call me when you get a chance. I've found some info on the burglaries."

"Yeah, it's a zoo here. I'll call you back." Harris hung up and Jeff slowly closed his phone. This was getting more serious all the time.

Jeff headed to his house. MJ would be tied up for at least another hour. He debated whether to call her with his new info, but decided it could wait until she could discuss it with him. It wasn't going to go away.

Chapter 18

Jeff parked his car in the garage. He hit the remote to close the door and went into the house through the inside door. He hit the lights, pulling off his jacket as he walked through the kitchen. He hung his jacket in the closet, threw his tie on the dresser and fixed himself a drink back in the kitchen. He was too worn out to think about fixing anything for dinner. If MJ hadn't eaten, they could run down to Tally's and get something.

With all the crap that was going on, he thought it was time that he and MJ started packing iron. Under normal circumstances, it wasn't necessary unless they were on a protection detail, but this sure as hell wasn't normal. He headed down to the basement. He had a gun safe there. He entered the combination and swung open the door. His favorite was the .45 Colt, the old tried and true 1911 model. He kept one at the office and one here. Both had been accurized and had trigger jobs. He pulled the auto along with two spare magazines out of the safe. He picked up an inside the pants holster to carry it in. MJ's favorite was the Glock .40. He took her gun out too, along with two loaded magazines and her favorite holster. She liked to wear one on the waist, and she always wore a jacket with it. It was the way she had carried as an agent and it worked for her. Both she and Jeff practiced weekly and enjoyed shooting in combat matches. The trophies along the basement wall were proof of their expertise.

He took the guns to the workbench. He field stripped them, cleaned them and reassembled them, one at a time. He took out ammo for each gun and loaded the magazines. He used the high shock hollow point loads. They both were expert reloaders and reloaded their own ammo for targets and competition shoots. For serious street work, they used the factory stuff, usually the Federal brand 'Hydra-Shok', potent and accurate. Two magazines for the Glock, three for the Colt. The Glock held fifteen rounds in the magazine, compared to seven for the Colt. If they needed more than that, they were in serious trouble.

Jeff put the guns in the holsters and took them upstairs. He put the pistols along with the extra magazines on the dining room table. He considered them for a minute, and then went back to the basement. He selected two pump shotguns and two boxes of double ought buck. They could each put one of the pump guns in the trunk of their cars. Short of explosives, they should have enough firepower. He thought again about the grenade that had been tossed at him. Too bad he didn't have a box of them for each car also.

Jeff looked at his watch, just now 5:30. He figured he had time for a quick shower before MJ got home. She would probably want a shower before they went to Tallys tonight. He headed back to the bedroom and threw his clothes in the hamper. He hung his sport coat in the closet. He jumped in the shower and let the hot spray beat on his head and shoulders. It helped relieve some of the tension he had built up. He shut the shower off before he used all the hot water. Better save some for MJ. He ran the electric razor over his face and trimmed his mustache and goatee. He sprayed on some deodorant and splashed some aftershave on his face. He walked back into the bedroom and picked out a dark shirt and pair of pants to match. He picked out a sport coat that went with the ensemble and put on his soft black Pikolinos loafers.

Jeff went back into the living room and turned on the TV. He got the six o'clock news on and sat back to watch while he waited for MJ.

Chapter 19

MJ arrived at the house just as the news was signing off. There had been no mention of any of their episodes, but the news of the two bodies found in the lake was announced, even though skimpy on information. There were some clips of the bodies being loaded in the ambulance and a short interview with Captain Harris. John looked tired and drawn in the interview. Jeff could well imagine he had been through the mill with the chief and the mayor pressing for action on the burglaries and now this.

MJ hopped in through the doors and dropped her purse on the table with all the weapons. She came directly to Jeff and gave him a big hug. "I was so worried about you."

Jeff returned the hug, then held her at arms length. "I'm fine. You O.K.?"

"I'm good, a little frazzled after dealing with that jerk agent again." She went back over by the table and surveyed the arsenal laid out there.

Her eyebrows raised, she turned to Jeff. "We declaring war or something?"

"You know how the saying goes, 'help fight crime, shoot back', so I think we ought to be ready." Jeff got up from the couch and kissed MJ, holding her lightly by the elbows. "You want to do Tally's tonight?"

"Sounds great, but I'm going to hop in the shower first, I feel grubby." MJ headed back towards the bedroom, kicking off her shoes as she walked towards the bed. She sat down on the edge of the bed and started removing her clothes. Jeff stood in the doorway watching, a smile on his face.

"Forget it." MJ grinned at him. She continued to strip, then walked past him towards the shower. Jeff gave her a gentle pat on her backside and went back to the living room. MJ went into the bathroom and closed the door. He could hear the shower come on.

Jeff went back to the living room. He hated being on the defensive. He had no idea who was behind the attacks and what their agenda was. He just knew he wanted to be ready for whatever they threw at him next. He wanted to hit back, and hard.

He fixed himself vodka and seven. He watched the stupid television program without comprehending what message they were trying to get across, if any. Some inane Hollywood thing. He sipped his drink and waited for MJ to get ready. His mind was still active, trying to figure out this latest crime wave.

MJ emerged from the bedroom, looking like a million bucks. She wore a simple black sheath dress that accentuated her figure. Jeff was mesmerized by the look. Just a simple dress, but she carried it off as if it were a designer original.

She came over to where Jeff was sitting on the sofa. He was sure his mouth was hanging open. She smiled and held her hand out to him. He held her hand and felt the electricity flow through him. He wanted to just hold her and forget all the crap that was going down. He did a mental shake, and they walked to the front door.

"Wonder what the special is at Tally's tonight?" MJ asked. Her favorite was the Asiago beef.

"I think, tonight is the all you can eat barbeque ribs." Jeff said, still taking in MJ's appearance. He could care less. Just being in the company of MJ made him feel like a king.

"Whatever, I'm starved." MJ led the way out to the garage.

"Whoops, wait a minute." Jeff went back into the house. He grabbed all the weapons from the table and carried them out to the car. He opened the trunk on both vehicles with his remote and put the shotguns and ammo in the trunks. He took the pistols to MJ's car and handed hers to her.

"You can put yours under the front seat." Jeff said as he put his Colt in his waistband. He put a magazine in each of his sport coat pockets and handed MJ the extra magazines for her Glock. "You can put your extras in the glove box for now."

MJ did as she was instructed. She realized what Jeff was preparing them for. She wasn't the type to argue with a valid threat. She did a quick check on her Glock and stuffed it in the glove box.

"I should have worn something more appropriate for carrying." She was checking the magazines and putting them in next to her pistol.

"It's worth it to me. You look fantastic. Screw these guys." Jeff smiled at her, completely enthralled with her ability to cope with the situation.

MJ smiled, and posed, which about threw Jeff into a seizure. "God! You look terrific!" Jeff exclaimed as he got into the driver's seat. He was starting to fantasize about the evening to come.

The drive to Tally's was without incident. Jeff told MJ about his findings that day. She thought he was really on to something. They threw ideas back and forth until they pulled up in front of Tally's.

Jeff parked in a spot directly in front of the restaurant. They seemed to be lucky that way; they almost always got the same spot. Jeff locked up the car and led MJ to the entrance. They checked the specials on the blackboard. Sure enough, Jeff had been right about the special, it was the 'all you can eat ribs' tonight.

They got their usual table in the bar. They could see the flat screen TV and everybody that was sitting at the bar. Austin was working behind the bar. He waved at them as they came in and started mixing their usual drinks. Nick was their waiter tonight. He came over with his usual smile and handed them the menus.

"Any questions you guys?" Nick knew they probably had the menu memorized. "Your drinks should be ready soon, any appetizer tonight?"

Jeff ordered the Tally chips, a local favorite; they made their own chips at the bar and served them hot with a ranch dip.

Nick brought their drinks and assured them the chips were on the way. "Ready to order?"

MJ gave him a look that Jeff knew would make Nick weak at the knees. "Special for me Nick."

Jeff responded with, "Same for me." wondering if Nick had recovered enough to get his order.

Nick gave them both a big smile and took off.

"You got to quit doing that." Jeff said, leaning towards MJ. "You're going to give that poor guy a heart attack."

MJ just smiled. She knew what affect she had. She didn't use it a lot, but some of it just came natural. "I like Nick. I think he likes me too."

"Well, duh, what make you think that? Maybe the way he drools when he looks at you?"

"I think you're exaggerating." MJ gave him a look.

Jeff let his mouth drop open, "Am I drooling yet?"

"Stop it, you look goofy." MJ laughed. It sounded good to hear her laugh. They had been through a tough week. MJ was taking it all in stride.

"Did you put the deal to Kelly and Roger?" Just then Nick returned with their drinks. He glowed at MJ again. "Your orders will be right out." Jeff could have been on another planet. Nick was totally in awe of MJ. Jeff didn't blame him.

MJ gave Nick another of those hundred watt smiles. He practically melted, then took off, nearly running into Kate, one of the other servers. Kate looked at Jeff and shook her head.

"Yes, I did. They both sound eager to help. They thought it would be a nice change of pace." MJ took a sip of her Cosmo. "They're coming in Monday morning to get all the details."

"Good. I'll feel a lot better with them on the job." Nick took a drink of his martini. Nobody made them as good as Austin; it was ice cold and as dry as it could be.

"Wow, you know what they say about martini's don't you?"

"No." MJ had heard this before, but she gave Jeff the chance to say it again.

"Two are too many, and three are not enough." Jeff grinned as he took another drink. He wouldn't have two tonight. Never knew what might happen later. He wanted to keep his edge.

They finished their meal and chatted with Robert, the owner. Nick, Austin and Kate stopped by for a few words. They finally paid their bill and headed out to the car.

Chapter 20

Jeff started the car and drove out of the parking. He was thinking about the evening ahead and didn't notice the pickup that followed.

He looked around as he got to the stop light and that's when he noticed the vehicle behind him.

"Heads up MJ. We might have company." MJ had enough moxie not to turn around, but she checked the side mirror.

"The pickup?"

"Yes, not sure, maybe I'm just paranoid." Jeff pulled his .45 out of his belt. MJ opened the glove box and got her Glock.

They drove several blocks, Jeff making some turns and changing speeds. The pickup stayed right behind them. MJ called the PD and gave them a heads up. Captain Harris had left word with the dispatcher to be alert for any calls from anybody connected with Hunter Security. The dispatcher put out a call for a car to head for their location.

Jeff was heading down Washington Parkway, a four-lane road that was well-lit. All of a sudden, the pickup pulled out and came up beside Jeff on the driver's side. Jeff had the .45 in his hand. He rolled the window down and got ready to hit the brakes. The pickup pulled even with them, then suddenly turned left at the intersection. Jeff kept going straight. That's when he noticed the black and white patrol car behind him. The car took off after the pickup truck, turning on his lights and siren. Jeff decided to tag along and see what transpired.

He could see the squad car had managed to pull the pickup over. An officer was getting out of the squad. No sign of movement in the pickup. Probably just a false alarm.

As the officer approached the truck, the door suddenly opened and the muzzle of a gun appeared in the gap. The cop drew his weapon, but never had a chance as he was sprayed with automatic fire from the truck. The squad car was a single man vehicle. The officer was down and the pickup sped off. MJ was already on the phone; Jeff stopped behind the squad car and got out to check on the cop.

There was a wound in the arm of the cop, but other than that, it appeared he was wearing his vest and several other rounds had been stopped by it. He had still taken the impact and had probably had the wind knocked out of him. Jeff kneeled down as the cop was attempting to get up.

"Better lie still for a minute, make sure you don't have any other injuries." Jeff was checking him over as he spoke. The young officer was obviously in pain, but his eyes were open and he appeared to all right other than the arm wound.

Jeff helped him to his feet and they walked back to the squad. He could hear sirens approaching. Jeff kneeled by the car and was applying a compression bandage he had gotten from the kit in the squad car.

An ambulance arrived first with another squad right behind it. Jeff directed the EMT to the wounded officer and MJ was talking through the window of the squad, giving the driver a description of the pickup and warned him about the automatic weapon. The officer drove off, his microphone in hand as he left.

Two more cars arrived at the scene, another squad and an unmarked car.

They were at the scene for another hour. They talked to the investigating officers and the detectives that showed up. They made arrangements to meet at the station the following day to sign statements. While they were talking to the officers, the lead detective got a call on the radio. The pickup had been found abandoned. A crew was headed to the site to examine the vehicle for evidence. The detective told Jeff that the Escalade involved in his altercation had also been found. It had been abandoned and burned. At least the pickup hadn't been burned. They both doubted there would be much evidence left behind.

MJ and Jeff finally got in their car and left. There were still a few officers searching the scene for any remaining brass from the automatic weapon. Several ejected rounds had already been found and would be kept to help identify the weapon, if and when it was found.

Chapter 21

They approached the house cautiously. There
was a squad parked in front and an officer waited for
them by the garage.

The officer introduced himself and told them he
would stick around until they were sure the house was
safe. They all walked through the house, checking
closets and anywhere a person could hide. Nothing
unusual was found.

They thanked the officer and he left, assuring
them there would be extra patrols in the neighborhood.

MJ had been carrying the Glock while they
searched the house. She put it in the nightstand on her
side of the bed, then flopped on top of the bed, one
hand covering her eyes. Jeff knew how she felt, he was
exhausted also. He lay down next to her and put an arm
around her. They held each other for a few minutes,
then MJ rolled off the bed and got to her feet.

"I'm going to call into the central station and give
them an update." She walked into the office and sat in
the chair. She dialed a number on the phone and leaned
back, putting her feet up on the desk.

Jeff followed her into the office. "Check and see if they've had any unusual activity at any of our accounts too."

MJ nodded and spoke into the phone. Jeff headed out to the kitchen. He opened the fridge and peered inside. He pulled out the milk carton and got a glass from the cupboard. "You want anything?" He yelled at MJ. He got a negative response, so he put the milk away and got a cookie from the bread box.

He went back in the office with his milk and cookie. MJ was still talking on the phone. He sat in the other chair and stretched out, kicking off his shoes. He sat the milk down on the floor and pulled the .45 from its holster and laid it on the corner of the desk. Picking up the milk, he took a drink and then a bite from the cookie.

He chewed on the cookie and washed it down with more milk. "Anything new?"

MJ hung up the phone and shook her head. "Just our little episode." MJ put her feet on the floor and stretched out her legs. She kicked her shoes off and rubbed Jeff's feet with hers.

"I'm still wired." MJ got up and went over to the file cabinet. She pulled open the top drawer and took out a folder. "I'm going to check our accounts. Make sure all this isn't about any of them."

"Good idea." Jeff finished his milk and got up also. "I've got a few things I want to run by you, see what you think." He headed back to the kitchen with his empty glass. "Be right back."

He came back to the office. MJ had the folder open, browsing through the paperwork inside. Jeff pulled his chair up next to hers. They went through the accounts, looking for anything that might catch their combined eyes.

"Here's something," MJ said, pulling a sheet from the folder. "Jacobs Jewelers is getting a shipment of loose diamonds for their annual sale." She handed the sheet to Jeff. "They don't have a specific time listed; they just wanted to give us a heads up."

"When did they send this?" Jeff was looking at the sheet. "I don't see a date on it."

MJ looked over his shoulder. "There it is, at the bottom. It came in last Wednesday; the shipment is due to arrive this week-end."

"How do their shipments come in?"

"They use a bonded courier that's based in Springfield at their home office." MJ handed Jeff another sheet. "Here's the info from their last shipment. They use the same outfit every time. Guess they don't trust the mail."

Jeff took the sheet. "Their problem. It's probably safer than a courier service. I can guarantee you it's cheaper. Registered mail is hand delivered, plus it's protected by the U.S. Postal Inspection Service."

MJ twirled a finger in the air. "Whoopee! Excuse me for forgetting your past employment. Probably not as safe now that you're no longer with them."

"Of course not, but it's still fairly reliable." Jeff grinned. "Kind of like the collapse of the F.B.I. after you left."

"Yeah, right. Do you think they even know that I'm gone?"

"Well yeah, at least I know the local office knows and misses you. You were their best looking agent, by far."

"Doesn't say much, does it? You remember those guys. Not exactly poster children, not to mention that I was the only female in the group."

"You miss it?"

"Sometimes. I miss the guys and the cases, sure don't miss the court time and the paperwork."

"Same here. Course, I never had the court time. That was the advantage I had, being a techie, I could give a deposition to the case officer, never had to testify in court."

"Lucky you. I remember that guy from the Justice Department. He came in to give us a lecture one time on court proceedings. He said it wasn't hard to catch the guilty party, the hard part was proving it in court."

They got back to the problem at hand. They bounced ideas off of one another; finally coming up with what they thought might be a solution.

"So everything has been running fairly normal, no big security issues until this week-end. Now we have everybody running around trying to cover these three projects. We seem to be the only link that ties them together." Jeff rubbed his eyes with his fists. "Just about has to be one of them. Our top priority, if you can prioritize these things, would be to keep tabs on Erikson. They're going to have a lot of firepower coming in this week-end. In the wrong hands, that could be disastrous."

"We have to cover Rebel Yell too." MJ put in, "If there's a kidnap attempt, it could be a disaster too." Jeff nodded agreement, "And of course the Jacob account could be in jeopardy, those diamonds will have a real market value, either on the legitimate market, or the not so legitimate market."

"We'll just have to cover them all." Jeff threw his hands in the air. "We can do it; it's just going to have us spread out pretty thin."

"Let's take a look at the maps and see if there's anything we've missed."

They got the maps out for a look.

Bloomington was a mid-sized city with two interstate highways bisecting it. There was a bypass that circled around the perimeter of the city and joined the two interstates at their junctions on each side. The airport was located on the south side of town. Most of the streets ran north and south, and east and west. There were four shopping malls, and a good number of strip malls located around the town.

Being the county seat, it had the sheriff's office, along with a fairly large police department. Several of the suburbs had their own police also. There were offices downtown for various state law-enforcement agencies as well as for the F.B.I., AT & F, DEA, TSA, and Homeland security. Customs and immigration had their own offices located near the mall on the north side of town.

Communications was broken into each agencies own frequencies, along with an emergency channel that all monitored. The main transmitters were located on the top floor of the Embassy building, with repeaters located around the city at strategic points. Cell phone coverage was good with all the providers having equal coverage.

Hunter Security was located near the center of the city. It was one of the newer companies providing security to the local businesses. As a result, their equipment was state of the art. Jeff's background had helped with that. He was strongly considering Bobby's recommendation to have a backup remote site for all their alarm and video monitoring. It would require some site reviews for a setting that was secure enough and cost was a factor also. He thought maybe he could set up the equipment in the basement of his house. He had a storage room that he could empty out and use. He'd have to run that by Bobby and get his input.

Shifting his attention back to the maps, Jeff noted all the different transportation accesses available. Amtrak had a station downtown, along with Greyhound bus. Besides the regional airport, there were four smaller airfields located around town. They could only handle small aircraft, but they could connect to the larger fields as well. The local airport had connections with most of the big airlines. Flight connections weren't as good as some of the larger fields, but they had a few direct flights to some of the more popular destinations.

If anybody wanted to pull a job here, they would have a lot of access to escape routes. The interstates gave them four options for direction of travel, and then there were the airlines, trains and buses to consider. The big factor was response time.

That was why the outfit had been pulling all these burglaries. Not so much for the loot, but to check on response time and how good the security systems were. According to Captain Harris, there had been over thirty burglary or burglary attempts made in the last month. That was one a day. There were probably a few that were other than the outfit that was after them, but that was still quite a few. Hunter Security accounts had been among the first, but the systems worked well there, and after the first week, the concentration had been on the other security company's accounts.

Jeff wished they would have picked one of them to concentrate their efforts. As it were, he'd have to make do with what he had. He took stock of the situation. He had a total of twenty employees. Fifteen full time, and five part time. He had two patrol vehicles that were on constant patrol, and one back up unit. Each car had one driver/operator and each car was equipped with a two way radio and a laptop computer. Each driver had a company cell phone. The drivers were not armed, although they did have a canister of mace, a taser, and a nightstick. All the drivers had training in unarmed combat and had to recertify annually. The drivers were also Red Cross trained in emergency medical procedures and were certified annually for that training also.

He had two of the part-time employees on board as executive protection specialists. They were both former police officers and had permits to carry weapons. They had taken the ASIS training for EPS and both had advanced training in unarmed combat.

Bobby and Marty would be running the office, with Bobby having the additional duties as the video and computer specialist.

MJ was a highly trained agent with the F.B.I. before she came to work with Hunter Security. She brought her expertise and contacts with her.

Jeff felt confident that he had the best personnel possible to handle any job that came up. All they could

do is wait and respond to whatever happened. He had a
hunch that the worse would be over after the week-end.

Chapter 22

Police captain John Harris was sitting in his office, reviewing the episodes of the last week. He had an officer in the hospital with a gunshot wound, a whole lot of burglaries and attempts, and several attacks on the citizens of his town. There were two dead goons in the morgue. He wanted it all to end. To top it all off, he had very few leads to follow. The brass casings recovered at the shooting were in the state crime lab. He hoped to get the results of the tests back soon. A fingerprint would be nice.

He had detectives working on the background of the two ex-cons that were in the morgue. Neither of them had any family or friends in the area. Both were from Michigan, and had apparently left that part of the country about a year ago. No record of their whereabouts since then.

The pickup truck used in the attack on the officer had turned up no new leads either. It had been carefully wiped down with what appeared to be Clorox bleach. The Cadillac Escalade had been burnt to a charred heap. No leads there either.

His information from Jeff Hunter had been helpful in figuring out the 'why' of the burglaries, even though the 'who' was still a mystery.

Harris had his officers working their CI's to try to find out what was going on in the underworld in the city. Nobody knew, or wasn't saying, what was going on. All Harris had was a big zero, and pressure from the chief and the mayor to make it stop.

He looked at the pile of paperwork on his desk. He had a good idea what he would be doing this week-end.

Chapter 23

The phone on the bed stand rang at 4:30 a.m. It was on Jeff's side of the bed. He picked it up and listened.

"Jeff! Bobby here. Somebody threw a grenade into the office." Jeff was instantly awake.

"Was anybody hurt? How bad is it?"

"Nobody was hurt. The front office is a mess, but the central station is o.k. We're still functioning."

"I'll be right there. Are you at the office?"

Bobby was talking to somebody off line. "What? Yes, I'm here at the scene. The police and fire departments are here too."

"Good. See you real soon." Jeff hung up the phone and jumped out of bed. He was pulling his pants on when MJ sat up in bed. "What's going on?"

Jeff filled her in. She jumped out of bed and started dressing too. "We better take both cars, hard telling what will be going on."

They finished dressing at the same time. They shared the sink at the bathroom, doing a quick wash and brush, grabbed their pistols from the bed stands, and then headed for the garage.

They headed for their cars as Jeff hit the remote to open the garage doors. As the door swung up, Jeff saw two figures standing on the drive. The outside light had come when he hit the remote, and both men were caught in the glare. Jeff could see they were armed with some kind of long gun.

"Look out MJ!" he shouted. He was swinging his pistol up as he yelled. He hadn't had a chance to holster it; it was still in his hand. He fired two quick shots at each figure. MJ's Glock fired at the same time. Both men went down.

Jeff kept his Colt pointed at the men as he approached. One was still; the other was moaning and rolling around. Jeff kicked the guns away, noting that they were sawed off pump shotguns. MJ approached from her side of the garage, pointing her Glock at the one that was still moving.

The still figure had a head wound, right between the eyes. It made no difference if it was the .45 Colt, or the .40 Glock. Either meant that this one was gone.

The one that was making the noise and rolling around had a shoulder wound and one in his thigh. Jeff could see marks on both men's chests that indicated hits. Apparently they were wearing vests. Vests didn't stop head shots, or shots to the limbs though.

MJ had her cell phone out as Jeff knelt down by the wounded man. The shoulder wound didn't look too serious, but the wound in the thigh was bleeding profusely. Jeff pulled the man's belt from his pants and wrapped it around the thigh above the wound. He took his ball point pen and wrote the time on the man's forehead. The EMT's would want to know how long the tourniquet had been in place.

MJ did a quick search of both men. Neither had any identification. Both had a small roll of bills in their pockets. Both were dressed in dark clothes, black jeans, sweaters and jackets of a matching dark material. Both had black watch caps. Jeff examined one. It had eye holes and could be pulled down over the face.

117

Jeff's ears were ringing from the shots. His first reaction had been to check to see if MJ was all right. They had been lucky. This attempt was probably tied to the grenade at the office. These two had the bad luck to approach the house after Jeff and MJ had been alerted. He doubted if it had been planned that way.

He heard sirens, then saw a patrol car heading their way, lights blazing. Another patrol car was coming from the other direction. Jeff and MJ placed their weapons on the back of Jeff's car and stood out in the light with their hands out in plain sight.

The officers approached slowly, weapons at the ready. Jeff recognized both of them. As they got closer, they recognized Jeff and MJ and lowered their weapons. "What's going on Jeff?"

It was Bob Delaney, an old timer and sergeant on the night shift.

"Hi Bob, these two were coming after us, but we surprised them." Jeff pointed at the two on the ground. "This one has a bleeding thigh wound and a shoulder wound." He indicated the one with the tourniquet. "This one is d-dead, with a hole in his head."

Delaney grinned. "You a poet?"

Jeff shook his head. He hadn't meant to be funny.

"There was an explosion at our office. We got a call a few minutes ago and were headed there when we met these two."

"I know, we were at the scene. You've got a mess to clean up." Delaney was kneeling by the wounded man.

"Got any idea who these two are?" He asked. "Sure don't look familiar to me."

"None. Never seen them before." Jeff responded.

"You two will have to stick around until the shift captain can get somebody here to process the scene. I imagine they're on their way now." Delaney motioned to the younger officer. "Glen, you secure the area. I'm sure we're going to have some gawkers. Don't want them trampling up the scene."

"Right Bob." Glen headed towards his vehicle to get his crime scene kit.

By this time, the ambulance had arrived and the EMT's were working on the wounded man. "We have to take this one in right away, he's bleeding pretty badly." The first EMT said to Bob.

"Let me cuff him first." Delaney pulled a pair of handcuffs from his belt.

"Hold it a sec; I need to finish wrapping this shoulder wound. It's not that bad, more of a graze than anything. It's that leg wound that's the problem."

The EMT had removed the man's jacket and shirt. He bandaged the wounded arm and watched as Delaney put the cuffs on him. Another EMT was working on the thigh wound. She had cut away the pants leg and had a compression bandage on the thigh. She replaced the belt with her own tourniquet.

The wounded man had lost consciousness and wasn't moaning or rolling around anymore. They put him on a gurney and rolled him towards the ambulance.

"I'll have a man meet you at the emergency entrance." Delaney called after them, pulling his mike. He spoke into the mike, then turned back to MJ and Jeff.

"You guys want to go inside. I'll have Glen stand by here until we can get some more help." A small crowd had already started to gather on the sidewalk. The sergeant motioned MJ and Jeff towards the house and then headed down to the walk to help his officer keep the crowd back.

MJ was talking on her cell phone again. Jeff picked up their guns and they went back into the house. He put the guns on the kitchen counter. The officer working the case would probably need to take them until they got the interviews over with.

MJ was still on the phone, so Jeff started making coffee. He could see more police cars pulling up at the curb. There was crime scene tape around the driveway.

Chapter 24

Carter sat at the table with the crew. He did a mental assessment of each one. He saw several weak links. He usually didn't work with a crew, but the payoff on this job sounded too good to pass up. He'd give it a few more days. Arquet was experienced; he knew that from the stories and rumors that had floated around about him. He had heard about him when he was doing time in Joliet. The inmates talking about him acted like he was some kind of god. Carter had to give him credit. If he could pull this job off, they'd all be sitting pretty.

There were eight of them total. Carter was here because of his skills as a burglar. The ones he considered weak links were the strong arm boys. They were long on brawn, but short on brains. The way he had it figured, Arquet would consider them expendable. If somebody had to be sacrificed, they'd make good ones.

Carter had been pulling burglaries around the city to check response time and the level of expertise of the installations and the responders. It was just as Arquet had figured. Hunter Security was the top dog. The other systems varied in the degree of security provided, anywhere from zero to pretty good. Hunter's systems were the toughest. Even Carter couldn't get past them. He had ideas on how to overcome their systems, but the risk involved was high.

Arquet was standing at the front of the room, using a pointer and a map on a wall to give directions to the crew that was going out that night. The way Arquet had it figured; they needed to disrupt Hunter Security's operations in order to hit their main targets.

Anders and Snelling were going to try to kidnap Mary Jo Conrad, known as MJ. If they could hold her someplace, they'd have leverage on Jeff Hunter. She was also instrumental in the running of the business and the head of their executive protection detail. She wouldn't be an easy target. They all knew of her background, and Arquet had stressed that they didn't underestimate her.

Carter watched the three of them. Arquet was going on and on about how tough that little gal would be, but he could tell that Anders and Snelling weren't buying it. They both had a half sneer on their puss as they exchanged glances and nods. They kept saying, "Yeah, yeah" but Carter knew they thought Arquet was a wuss. Not his problem.

There were other plans on the table too. Possibly a hit on Jeff Hunter, maybe trying to knock out the central station or maybe roughing up some of the employees. They needed to keep Hunter Security off balance until the job was done. Carter had some ideas of his own, but nobody asked him.

Usually when Carter pulled a job, he first got as much info about the layout of the target as he could. He would go online, find out the hours of operation, who the employees were, and even get the floor plan of the building. He could find out what security company, if any, was in charge of their alarms. Once he knew that, he could figure out how to bypass them.

He worked alone if he could, and if not, he'd get some help from a known source. That's what bugged him about this job. He didn't know any of the others. All he had was what they said they could do. It made him nervous. The burglary jobs he had pulled off here in this town had gone well and he had to admit, the times he had to use some of these guys, they had performed pretty well. They seemed pretty solid, but he still wasn't sure how they'd do when the pressure was on.

Chapter 25

Arquet was furious. Anders was whining about how they were ambushed, and Snelling was sniveling about their injuries. The little ex-F.B.I. gal had whupped their asses. It was all Carter could do not to break out laughing. The two of them had been lucky to get away. Arquet was upset because they had tipped their hand. It would be difficult to surprise them now.

"I'm giving you two assholes one more chance." Arquet stood in front of them. Snelling was sitting in a chair holding his damaged knee while Anders was leaning on the back of the chair, his face still contorted from the kick he had received in the crotch. Their cockiness was gone.

"Try to see if you can put a hurt on their technician, Bobby Cantor." Arquet was trying to control his temper. "He's a little guy, and a geek. Shouldn't be a problem, even for you two girl scouts."

Anders face was red. He had never been beat up by a woman before. He wanted to hurt somebody and bad. Snelling wasn't much happier. He wanted another shot too. He really wanted to grab that gal. Next time around, he'd show her, and show her good. She had surprised him with a lucky shot, that was all.

Chapter 26

Carter knew this was serious. Arquet was too quiet. He sat there listening to Anders and Snelling trying to tell him how they had screwed up again. The little techie guy had turned the tables on them once again. Anders and Snelling probably hadn't had such a bad day their entire lives. First a little gal kicked their ass, then they get tasered and maced by a geek.

Arquet was pacing the floor. Anders and Snelling were sitting in their chairs, looking at the floor. You could almost smell trouble. When Arquet walked behind them, he pulled out a pistol and shot both in the head. Bang! Bang!

Everybody sat still, frozen and unbelieving what had happened. Arquet put the pistol back in his shoulder holster and looked around the room. His face was a mask of fury.

"This is what happens when you fuck up." He looked each man in the eye. He walked back to the front of the room and leaned on the desk. "We have a job to do. And I want it done right." His voice was just over a whisper.   Even with their ears ringing from the shots, every man heard his every word.

Chapter 27

Carter was glad his job was relatively safe. He had too much experience to screw it up. He didn't have an inflated ego or a sense that he was better at what he did than anybody else. What he did was a career option. He was good at it, probably better than most, but he knew that even with his knowledge and experience that shit happened. He only had one stretch in the joint. Back when he was younger and thought he knew everything. He had taken chances back then. After serving his time, he swore he'd never be that stupid again. So far, he had been right. Now, he was having second thoughts. This was too intense.

Arquet and Carter were the only two in the room. Arquet sat behind his desk, and Carter sat on a straight chair in front of the desk. The desk was covered with maps and schedules.

"What do you think, Carter? Can we pull this off?" Arquet sat back in his swivel chair and eyed Carter.

"I think we have a really good chance. It will all boil down to timing. We have to get in and out within our set range. That's the only way we can beat the response time." Carter was relaxed. Looking at him, you would have thought they were discussing what to have for dessert.

"Timing is of the essence." Arquet was making his point by jabbing the map with his index finger. "I'm leaving that part up to you. It's the most important segment of the whole operation. I still think it would help if we could get some kind of hold on Hunter. They're more of a problem than the law."

Carter agreed, but he didn't want to press it much further. It was drawing too much attention, and as they had found out, it wasn't an easy operation.

To pull off a big job like this, they needed a diversion. Something that would distract not only the police, but Hunter Security as well. It should also be something that would disrupt travel and communications. Carter had pulled off jobs like that before, by starting a big fire, or creating a huge outage of power, and once by creating a huge traffic jam by wrecking a semi right at rush hour. He had all kinds of ideas for this job.

He didn't like working with this big of a crew. He preferred smaller jobs, maybe with a little less payoff, but with considerably less risk too. Most of his jobs were planned as much as a year ahead of time, and his crew consisted of a driver and combination helper/lookout. Usually three at the most. He knew his crew and he could trust them to do their job professionally. There were too many amateurs in Arquet's group.

He didn't care much for Arquet either. He had the impression that Arquet would be willing to sacrifice the whole crew if that's what it took to keep his skin whole. He had been too quick to dispatch Anders and Snelling. It wasn't necessary and it drew more attention to them. He could have put them on another assignment that wouldn't have involved as much brain as it did brawn. Carter spotted them both as potential weak links in the organization.

Chapter 28

Hunter and Bobby had gotten the office set up and they had set up a backup monitoring station in Jeff's basement. It looked like an impossible task at first, but once they got started, it didn't take long at all. Bobby was a whiz at running cable and hooking up the gear. Most of the gear they already had at the central station as backup. Putting it in a remote location made the backup more secure in case of a major disaster at the station.

For now, the remote site would have to be running unattended. That would work, as it was being duplicated at the central office anyway. If need be, they could pull personnel from the station to monitor at the remote. The hardest part had been getting the two way radio set up. In order to get enough range, they had to mount an antenna on the roof of Jeff's house. It was a temporary set up for now, but as time allowed, they'd make it permanent.

Chapter 29

Carter's team had set the explosives next to a big propane tank next to the building. The building was used for storage for materials for a construction company. Lumber, roofing materials and paints were stored there. It was a large two story building with offices in the front part, next to the parking lot. The propane was used as fuel for their smaller delivery vans. The site was located partially under the overpass for the interstate.

It was 3 a.m. They had the explosives pretty well hidden behind an inspection panel next to the big tank. The panel was a junction box for the electrical controls for the tank. Carter set the timer for 5 p.m. that afternoon. Rush hour traffic should be just about at its peak on the interstate above at that time. He smiled to himself as he envisioned the mess and confusion that would cause. It should be good distractions for their other pursuits and should keep things tied up for several hours.

Chapter 30

MJ was with Roger and Kelly. Rebel Yell was setting up their equipment in the auditorium. They wanted to try out everything before the concert. The sound crew had arrived in a van with the equipment on their truck. They had started setting up even before Rebel Yell's flight had landed. They were putting the finishing touches on it now.

MJ was overseeing the stage setup. Roger and Kelly were with the band. Fans had been arriving long before the concert was due to start. It kept Roger and Kelly busy keeping them away from the band until they could get them locked away inside. MJ had helped with the arrival, but she wanted to check the auditorium too. She was familiar with the layout. They had provided escort service for other bands in the past. She walked the perimeter first, checking all the doors to make sure they were all secure. All doors except the main entrance were alarmed. They were emergency exits only. The auditorium had their own security, but MJ liked to double check.

It was four hours before the concert was to begin. Once the crew had the equipment set up, Rebel Yell would do a quick rehearsal, then they'd all break for a meal and short rest before coming back to perform. Everybody had done this so often, it was second nature to them. So far, everything had gone smooth as silk.

Chapter 31

The courier had just loaded the boxes containing Jacobs diamond shipment in his truck. The manager of the main office was standing by, nervously wringing his hands. The courier consisted of a driver and a guard. The truck was an armored panel truck with a secure container with a time lock inside the van.

The driver was loading the boxes while the guard stood by. He slammed the door shut on the rear of the van and secured all the locks on the doors. He smiled at the manager and signed the invoice for the shipment. He folded his copy and put it in his binder. The manager managed a weak smile in return and took his copy from the driver. He headed back into the store as the van pulled away from the curb. Neither noticed the SUV that pulled out after the van and followed at a discrete distance.

Chapter 32

The semi driver checked his mirrors and spotted his partner in the semi behind him. They had been driving as a convoy on this trip. He wasn't used to having an armed guard sitting in the cab with him. Usually on these runs, the drivers just made the deliveries. Since this was the first trip to the new facility, Erikson International, the company decided to be more careful.

He checked the mile marker. They were about 200 miles from their destination. Less than four hours, but both drivers were about due for a break. They'd make a stop at the usual truck stop for a quick coffee and pottee break. He looked over at the guard. He was asleep again. No big deal, this was a pretty boring run. They had run out of conversation after the first hour. They didn't have much in common to talk about.

Neither the drivers nor the guards noticed the passenger van that was following the rear semi. It had been there for the last twenty miles, driving the same speed, about four car lengths back. There were four large men in the van, all dressed in dark coveralls, all focused on the semi's in front of them.

Chapter 33

MJ was walking next to Donnie Young, the lead
singer for Rebel Yell. Kelly was several paces in front of
them and Roger was bringing up the rear. Roger and
Kelly had already escorted the band to the shuttle van
for the ride to the hotel. Krug, the agent was talking to
Donnie as they were walking down the hall. They were
going over the final details before the concert that night.

As they approached the exit, doors opened on
either side of the hall, one in front of them, and one
behind them. Two men stepped out of each door. Kelly
was hit with a taser and went down. At the same
instant, Roger was tasered from behind, and he also
went down. The other man behind them aimed a taser
at MJ, but just as he pulled the trigger, MJ went flat to
the floor, the taser darts passing where she had been.
The darts hit Krug, and he let out a yelp and went down
also. The two front men grabbed Donnie and hustled
him out the exit door, while the two men behind went
for MJ. She was flat on her back and Krug had fallen half
across her, pinning her to the floor.

As she struggled to get up, one of the men put a
stun gun to her neck and gave her a zap. Her head

138

bounced off the concrete floor and everything went black.

Chapter 34

The courier driver and the guard were having an argument about Bret Favre's return from retirement and going to the Vikings. As luck would have it, the driver was a Vikings fan, and the guard was a Packer fan. They were driving on a little used service road that let them bypass most of the traffic and lights in town. Things were going hot and heavy when an old pickup pulled out from a side street and stopped right in front of the van.

The driver looked up in time to see there was nobody in the pickup, just before he collided with it. Both airbags deployed. The guard had been sitting sideways in his seat and the airbag knocked him back against the dividing wall of the van, stunning him. The driver was fighting his airbag, trying to get it out of his face when both front doors of the van were yanked open. The driver and the guard were both hit with tasers. They were both stunned and sat semi-conscious in their seats. Men on either side of the van slipped flex-cuffs on both of them, then wrapped them to their seats with duct tape. Another man took the weapon and keys from the guard and headed to the rear of the van. He opened the back doors and slapped a small putty like substance on the lock of the box inside. He stuck a small stick the size of a pencil in the putty, and then let the doors slightly close. He ran back behind the SUV that had pulled up behind the van and pressed a button on a small box in his hand.

There was a muffled blast in the van, and the doors blew open with a cloud of grey smoke. The man ran back to the van, and reached inside the now open box and pulled out the boxes with the diamond shipment and loaded them in the back of the SUV.

All three men got in the SUV and it peeled out around the van. Two cars had stopped and the drivers were running towards the van as the SUV disappeared down a side street and out of sight.

Chapter 35

The guard woke up as the semi driver pulled into the lot of the truck stop. He stretched and yawned and looked at his watch. "Potty break?"

"Yep, and just in time." The driver was putting on the brakes and reached for his door handle. "I gotta go bad."

The second semi had parked next to them in the lot. The driver and guard in that semi followed the first two into the truck stop. They were exchanging jokes and grins as they entered the building.

The van with the four large men parked near and the men got out and followed the men from the semis into the building. The first pair headed straight for the men's room. The other driver and guard went to the café counter and took a seat. Two of the large men followed the first pair into the restroom, while the other two stood by the magazine rack, leafing through the magazines on display.

In the restroom, the driver headed for a urinal, while the guard went into one of the stalls. There was another man washing his hands, but other than that the room was empty. The driver finished taking a leak and went to the wash basin as the other man was leaving. One large man followed him out and pulled a sign that said, 'Out of Order' from his coveralls and stuck it on the door. He let the door close and then locked it from the inside. The driver hadn't noticed any of this; he was drying his hand s under the air dryer when he was tasered. He fell to the floor with a small shout and was instantly tied up with flex cuffs around his wrists and ankles. Duct tape went over his mouth.

The guard in the stall flushed the stool and was fumbling with his pants when he heard the driver fall. "Andy? You o.k.?" He said, unlocking the door.

As he opened the door, he was also tasered and got the same treatment as the driver. The two large men dragged them into the last two stalls and sat them on the stools. They jammed the doors shut and peeled off the coveralls, revealing that they wore the uniforms of the trucking company, just like the two men they had overpowered.

In the restaurant, the driver looked back towards the restroom. "Wonder what's taking them so long." He asked the guard that was sitting next to him. The guard mumbled a reply around a mouth full of toast and eggs, and kept shoveling in more food. The driver took a sip of his coffee and got up. "I'm going to go check." He got up and headed towards the restroom. One of the big men followed him and as they got near the door, as the driver paused to read the sign, the big man pushed him inside where the other two gave him the treatment and put him in another stall next to his friends.

The guard finished his meal and looked back towards the restroom. No sign of the others, just a large man by the magazine rack. He got up to go check the restroom. He wound up in the fourth stall.

The four large men, now dressed as the drivers and guards, headed out to the semis. As they pulled out of the truck stop, the guard in the rear semi leaned out the window and pushed a red button on a small box in his hand. The passenger van exploded with a huge flash of flame, starting a fire at the truck stop. The semi's continued down the road, then turned off on a ramp that led to the interstate, but heading the opposite direction they had been going.

Chapter 36

Jeff and Bobby were back in the office. Jeff felt good about the work they had accomplished. Once he had Kelly and Roger working as guards, he thought they'd be pretty safe from any more attacks and with the backup system, they'd be able to keep tabs on all their accounts, regardless what happened at the office.

"I'm going to have a cup of coffee, want one?" Jeff said to Bobby, as he headed towards the break room.

"Nah, I'm good." Bobby was testing the network router for the office. He was sitting at the terminal that received the alarms from the accounts. Everything was running smoothly.

The red phone that went directly to the police dispatcher rang. Bobby answered it immediately. When it rang, it meant trouble.

"Hunter Security." He said, grabbing a pencil and tablet. As he listened, his mouth dropped open. He hung up the phone and turned towards the break room.

"Jeff, Jeff! We got problems!"

"What?" Jeff was running back to the central station, slopping coffee as he ran.

"PD just called. MJ and crew were attacked. Donnie was kidnapped."

"Where are they? Are they all right?" Jeff sat the half empty cup on the counter.

"They're o.k, they were tasered. MJ called the PD as soon as she could, she was knocked unconscious. They have her at the emergency room, but they said she would be alright, just a minor concussion."

"Good God, thanks for that! How about Roger and Kelly?"

"Same deal. They were attacked all at once with tasers and stun guns."

"Holy shit. Guard the fort, I'm heading over to the emergency room. I've got to check on MJ."

"Go!" Bobby said, "I'll call you if anything else comes in here."

Jeff ran out of the building and jumped in his car. He was squealing tires as he left. He had just hit the street to the hospital when his cell rang.

"This is Hunter." He held the phone in his right hand as he steered with his left.

"Jeff, all hell has broke loose." It was Captain Harris.

"I know, I'm heading to the hospital now." Jeff said.

"It's not just about MJ and the kidnapping, the courier from Jacobs has been hijacked, and the trucks delivering the weapons to Erikson were taken too."

"Jeezus! What's going on?" Jeff was pulling into the emergency parking lot. He kept the cell phone to his ear as he got out of the car and started running to the emergency entrance.

"Not sure, but we've got all of our units running, along with the feds, the state troopers and the county. We had an explosion at Building Materials, right under the interstate. Big twenty car pileup. Happened right at five o'clock. The fire is still going and there might be more explosions if the paint materials inside get ignited." Harris sounded as harried as he must be. "I wanted to check base with you to see if you've had any alarm activity while all this is going on."

"Nothing yet, at least not up to the point when I left the office."

"Thank God for small favors." Harris responded. "With all of our troops tied up, our response time is going to be squat."

"I'll pass the word to our patrol cars, have them keep their eyes and ears open."

They concluded their call and Jeff ran up the steps into the emergency room. He got directions at the desk and headed back to the ICU. As he rounded the corner, he saw Kelly sitting in a wheelchair, talking to a doctor. He rushed up to them. "How you doing Kel?"

"Hey Jeff, I'm fine, just talking to doctor Sneider here. They want to keep MJ overnight for observation. She banged her head when she went down."

Jeff turned to the doctor. "How bad is it?"

"Not too bad at all, it's just that she had a concussion when she hit her head. It's better if she can remain here overnight so we can monitor her condition. She should be fine in the morning."

Jeff felt a surge of relief. "That sounds fine with me. Just take good care of her, o.k.?"

Dr. Sneider smiled, "We plan to do our best."

Kelly took his arm. "MJ's in this room here" He pointed. "Roger is getting released right now. I've got to be wheeled out, but I'm alright."

"Get Roger and come back here to MJ's room. I'd like to bring you all up to speed on what's going on."

Jeff shook hands with the doctor and headed into MJ's room. Kelly was being wheeled to the desk by a nurse. Jeff saw Roger at the desk, signing some papers. He waved and Jeff waved back. He went into MJ's room.

It was dark in the room except for a night light and a little light coming in around the shades that were drawn over the windows. MJ lay on the bed. She looked small and frail under the covers. She had an IV attached to one arm and some wires ran from under her covers to

149

a monitor by the bed. Soft beeps came from the monitor. MJ lay with her eyes closed.

Jeff walked softly over to the bed. MJ opened her eyes and smiled at him. "Hi boss."

"Jeez, MJ, you scared the shit out of me." Jeff took her free hand and squeezed it gently.

She squeezed back. "I'm o.k., got a bit of a headache from banging my head on the floor. I still twitch from the taser too. Can't believe I got taken down like that."

"You weren't the only one." Jeff said as Roger and Kelly came in the door. The nurse had made them stay in wheelchairs. They about filled the room when they all got inside.

Jeff sat down in the chair next to MJ's bed. Roger and Kelly wheeled themselves to the foot of the bed.

"Any word on Donnie?" MJ asked, a look of worry crossing her face.

"Nothing yet, but I'm sure we'll get a call. I'll see if anybody has contacted any of the crew or his agent."

"His agent is in here too, someplace." MJ said. "He took a hit from a taser and the doctor said it affected his heart somehow or another. They've got him in intensive care. Don't think he's conscious yet."

Jeff shook his head. He filled them in on what he had heard from Captain Harris. They all were stunned.

Roger spoke first. "Holy cow, sounds like world war three starting up."

"I think all of these incidents the last month or so are connected." Jeff looked at all of them. "I'm not sure which of these today is the main target, and what was done as a diversion. The fire, I'm sure was started as a means of occupying the police and fire departments and creating confusion. All three attacks on our clients were done away from the secure areas. The diamonds were hit enroute, the weapons, the same scenario and the kidnapping was done before you could get to the vehicles, where you had some security and communications."

Jeff thought about the incidents. The main concern, of course, was Donnie. His safety was paramount. He was sure there would be a ransom demand, and soon. The diamonds and the weapons were insured. The weapons were traceable, much more so than the diamonds. Loose diamonds were as good as cash. They could be bartered anywhere. If the weapons could be transported out of the country, you could kiss them goodbye. His best bet was that they were headed for Mexico. The drug cartels were paying top dollar for weapons of all kinds.

Jeff had to head back and contact Jacobs, Erikson and Rebel Yell. He had to assure them that Hunter Security was doing all it could to help recover their goods. Technically, he wasn't responsible for Erikson or Jacobs losses, as they were in transport and covered by other companies, but he still felt he should offer all the assistance he could, just as good customer relations.

The kidnapping was a different matter. Donnie had been under their protection and had been kidnapped in spite of that. He was directly responsible for that. The company was bonded, but it went beyond that. It was a personal thing with Jeff, especially since MJ and two of his best employees had been attacked. He wanted Donnie back, and he wanted to get the ones responsible for it.

Chapter 37

Carter was back at the 'office', as Arquet called it. He had been with the crew that got the diamonds. He was satisfied with the performance of the men with him and with the operation as a whole, at least, his part of it. He was not satisfied with the kidnapping.

Donnie was tied up to a chair. He was blindfolded and had a gag over his mouth. Carter looked at him, and at the two men guarding him. He shook his head. "Where's Arquet?"

The bigger of the two, nodded back in the direction of a closed door.

Carter walked over to the door and opened it. Arquet was leaned back in a chair, a big grin on his face. He motioned for Carter to sit down. Carter remained standing.

"What are you going to do with him?" He motioned towards Donnie in the chair.

"Probably going to swap him for a million bucks or so." Arquet stuck a cigar in his mouth, bit off the end, and spit it on the floor. He pulled a gold plated lighter

153

from his pocket and ran the flame up and down the cigar before lighting it. He took a puff on the cigar and blew a smoke ring.

Carter just watched him. His arms folded across his chest.

"What we pulled off was risky enough. We don't need a kidnapping rap to deal with."

Arquet just kept the grin pasted on his face. Carter was getting fed up with this clown.

"Have you told the big boss what you've done?"

Now Arquet blew up. He pounded his fist on the desk. "Just who the hell do you think you are, telling me what to do?" He had lost the grin and his face was a red mask of fury. "I'm running this show, not you, not anybody else."

Carter just nodded. He turned and walked out of the room. Arquet's voice followed him. "I don't need some two bit punk telling me how to run this show." Arquet was screaming now. Carter heard him slam his chair back and stomp out after him.

Arquet grabbed him by the shoulder and swung him around. Carter hit him with a solid right. It picked Arquet off his feet and he fell on his ass. His eyes were crossed momentarily, then he shook his head and started to get up. Carter hit him again and Arquet rolled across the floor. The rest of the crew just stood around watching, some were openly smiling to see Arquet get his mouth slapped shut.

Arquet rolled back around, his hand coming out from beneath his coat, a black automatic in his fist.

Carter had already pulled his by the time Arquet got turned around. He sent two quick shots into Arquet's chest. Arquet got a look of shock on his face as the gun in his hand drooped towards the floor. Carter took aim and put a third shot right between the eyes. A mess of blood and gore splashed across the floor. Arquet flopped once and lay still.

Nobody had moved. Carter looked around the room. All eyes met his, and several of the men nodded in approval. Slowly, they started to applaud, and soon every man in the room was applauding.

Chapter 38

Donnie was sitting very still, not knowing what was going on. He felt hands on his shoulders. Somebody was untying him. They left his hands tied and the blindfold on. The gag was removed. He ran his tongue around his dry lips. He tried to speak, but his mouth was too dry. He swallowed then tried again. "What's going on?"

Nobody answered, but hands were leading him across the room. He heard a door open and a pair of hands was leading him out of the building. He heard a car door open and then he was pushed into the back seat, his hands still tied and the blindfold still on. The car engine started and they took off down a bumpy street.

Carter watched them go from the second floor window. A couple of the guys were rolling Arquets body in a rug. They'd take it down to the river and dump it tonight. Probably wrap a couple of chains around it to sink it.

He called a meeting for that afternoon. He wanted to wait until he heard if the shipment of arms was on its way to Mexico. They had swapped tractors on the semi rigs and repainted the signs on the trailers. They were supposed to meet with their contacts in Nogales and do the exchange of guns for cash. They had a route all planned out to avoid the scales and DMV's check points. They should be arriving in Nogales the next day.

Arquet had played things close to his chest. Carter didn't know who he had been working for, but he was sure that he wasn't on his own; he wasn't smart enough for that. Carter planned on dividing up the take from the jewels, the weapons, and the burglaries he had pulled. If somebody from higher up came around, he'd worry about that then, until they did, he planned on making the split and moving on.

Donnie had been led out of the car. He still couldn't see, but from the amount of light that came around the blindfold, he figured they were either inside another building, or in a dark alley. He wasn't sure what to expect next, but he was ready to make a run for it. His hands were still tied, but his feet were loose. He still had a hand holding onto his arm. He was debating whether to shake loose and run, when a voice whispered in his ear.

"Just hang tight here buddy. We're going to set you loose. No hard feelings." Just as Donnie started to relax, he felt the prongs of a stun gun on the back of his neck. The next thing he knew, he was laying on the ground, twitching. His hands had been untied, but he couldn't move. He heard footsteps running away, then the sound of a car engine starting up. As the sounds of the car faded away, he started to get feeling back in his arms. He reached up and pulled off the blindfold. It looked like he was in a parking garage. It was dark, but there were lights over a doorway some distance away. He headed that way, staggering at first, then getting his legs moving right, going a little faster. He got to the door and opened it. At first, he didn't know where he was, then he recognized it as the old bus terminal. It had been abandoned when they moved to a new location near downtown.

It was chilly, and he just had on the light jacket he had worn after the rehearsal. He looked at his watch. He could still make the concert tonight. The thought jarred him at first, but then he grinned. Why not? It would make for some fantastic PR!

Chapter 39

Jeff was talking to Captain Harris. They were going over the events of the day.

"Five o'clock. Everything went down right at five." Harris was shaking his head. "The fire, the hijack of the jewels, the hijack of the truck, and the kidnapping. All at five o'clock on the button!"

Jeff was shaking his head too. "The timing. It had to be done like clockwork. These guys were pros. Except for the kidnapping, I can't figure that. Too risky, sounds like an amateur move, even though they carried it off."

"Yeah, that part bothers me too." Just then Harris's phone rang. He picked it up. "Harris." He listened for a few minutes, then sat up straight. "You don't say! He's alright?" He looked at Jeff and covered the mouthpiece of the phone. "Donnie just turned up. He was let go out by the old bus depot."

Harris finished the conversation then hung up. "Go figure. Right when we were talking about it. I wonder if that was just an elaborate diversion or what?"

"Weird! Glad he's o.k., how was he taking it?"

"He wants to go on with the concert tonight. Said it was good PR for him. That ought to make Krug perk up and feel better." Harris leaned back in his chair.

"Now, if they'd just return the diamonds and the weapons, we can all go happily on our way."

"Don't hold your breath." Jeff didn't think that was happening. "I still want to whup some punk ass for what they did to MJ and the boys."

"Not to mention the grenade they threw at you." Harris was grim again. "This was too intense for just a hit and run job. A lot of planning went into this."

"I know they probably got some high value stuff, but there had to be quite a few individuals involved. The payoff won't be so much when it's split up. Those guys don't work for minimum wage."

"Maybe it's just a hobby thing." Jeff stood up. "Whatever, I've got to get back to the office. MJ's resting at the hospital. I'm going to check in with Bobby, then go over and see how she's doing. I'll probably check in with Rebel Yell and see what their plans are too. Roger and Kelly said they'd be back to work today, so maybe I'll let them go over and do their bodyguard thing again. I'd be willing to bet that nobody gets close again."

Harris barked a short laugh. "Count on it. If I know those guys, they're probably wishing somebody would try."

Jeff shook hands with Harris and headed out the door. "I'll check in again later." He waved and took off down the hall. He waved at a few acquaintances at the front desk, then went out to his car. He belted up and drove across town to his office.

He parked the car and walked to the front door of the office. They had put up one way plastic sheeting over the front windows. He couldn't see in, but anybody inside could see him. It made him a little nervous, but figured it would have the same affect on anybody else with malicious intent.

He pushed open the door, and Marty was sitting at the front desk. He noticed the pump shotgun half hidden by her chair. Marty looked up and grinned. "I saw you pull up. Just to be on the safe side, I got old Betsy out, but then I saw it was you."

"Good thinking Marty." Jeff walked down the aisle towards the central station in the rear. "Bobby back there?"

"Yep, he's been working his little butt off."

Jeff grinned and headed to the back. He swiped his card through the reader and put his finger on the biometric pad. There was a buzz, and he pulled the door open.

Bobby was at the console. He looked up as Jeff walked in.

"Hey Jeff, remember when Erikson first told us about that shipment coming in?" Bobby swung around in his chair to face Jeff.

"Yeah, I remember. You got together with some of his people right after that."

"Right. What I suggested was that they put some tracking beacons in the crates with the weapons."

Bobby had Jeff's full attention now. "And....?"

Bobby grinned. "They did. I called the beacons up and I've got them on the screen."

162

Jeff came over to the terminal. He could see some icons flashing on a map. They were heading southwest but he couldn't tell where they were. There was an arrow pointing north at the bottom of the screen. "Where are they?"

"Just leaving Kansas, heading south and west." Bobby zoomed out on the screen and Jeff could see that it was a map of the United States and the icons were located right at the Kansas Border.

"Whoopee!" Jeff said, "Better call the feds, this is interstate transportation of stolen goods."

"Already done that. I gave them the coordinates and they're closing in, as we speak." Bobby was grinning from ear to ear. "Somebody is in for a surprise."

Jeff and Bobby did a high five. Their yells had attracted the attention of the other two terminal monitors and even Marty stuck her head in the door. "What's going on?"

"Bobby here has tracked down the Erikson shipment."

163

Everybody cheered and they all exchanged high fives.

"Got to keep this line clear. The feds are communicating with me. I've got the only track on the trucks." Bobby swung back to his terminal.

"Good man Bobby. I'm going to give Captain Harris a call and give him the good news." Jeff started to leave, then turned back. "By the way, Donnie was turned loose by the kidnappers. He's planning on going ahead with the concert tonight. He acts like it was all a big joke."

Jeff went to his desk and called Captain Harris. He was relaying the good news about the weapons when Harris gave him some more news. "Donnie said that while they had him tied up and blindfolded, two of the kidnappers had an argument about the kidnapping and he heard some shots. That was right before they let him go. He guessed, probably right, that the one that was against the kidnapping won the argument."

"Looks like their operation is falling apart. I'm going back and see how the tracking is going with Bobby. They should be closing in any minute now."

164

"Keep me posted." Harris hung up.

Jeff went back to the central station. Everybody was standing around Bobby, listening in as he guided the feds to their rendezvous with the semis.

Bobby had the phone on speaker, so they were all quiet, listening to the exchange. The phone came to life. "Have them in sight. Agent Gordon, they're headed your way. Do you have the roadblock set up?" There were a couple of clicks then another voice came over the phone. "This is Gordon; we have a reception committee of six cars. Two of ours, and four state troopers. The road is closed and we're out of their sight, just over that rise about a half mile from your location." There was a pause, then the same voice came back. "We've closed the road and diverted all traffic. There is no traffic between us and the target."

There was another short pause then the first voice came back on over the phone. "Hunter Security, thanks for the info. We'll be taking it from here. I will contact you when we have made the stop."

Bobby picked up the phone. "This is Hunter Security. Keep us posted and you are very welcome."

He hung up the phone and clapped his hands together. "Got em!" Everybody cheered and clapped and high fived each other.

"Bobby, give me a jingle when all the dust has settled. I'm going over to see MJ and give her all the good news." Jeff squeezed Bobby's shoulder and trotted out to his car.

Chapter 40

˛ The drive over to the hospital was done in much better spirits than the first trip. It would be nice if they got the diamonds back too, make it a clean sweep. Jeff wasn't going to count on it. They had come out pretty well after all.

Jeff practically skipped down the hall to MJ's room. He eased open the door. MJ was awake and watching TV. She looked over and smiled when Jeff came in the room. "Hi lover!"

"Hi yourself, beautiful. Got some good news."

"I heard. They gave Krug the news, thought it might help him recover faster. It's helping, he's telling them he's alright and has to go back to the concert. Can you believe that Donnie?" MJ was shaking her head in disbelief.

"Yeah, how about that? But that's not all!" Jeff was grinning, holding back the latest. MJ looked at him, her eyes wide. "What?"

"We recovered the arms shipment." Jeff watched her eyes get bigger yet and her grin matched his.

"What? How? When?"

"Our boy Bobby had tracking devices in with the shipment. He was tracking them shortly after he found out about the hijack."

MJ squeezed his hand. "That's wonderful."

"The feds were making the bust just as I left. We should have all the details soon." Jeff squeezed back and MJ came into his arms and gave him a big hug.

"Get me out of here! I'm missing all the action." MJ sat up in bed. The IV had been disconnected and there was just a monitor line hooked to her arm. Jeff went to the closet and got her clothes.

"I'll get the doctor. I'm sure you're good to go by now." Jeff knew how MJ felt. It would be worse laying here than it would be out doing something. "Hang on a sec. We have to get you disconnected from the monitor."

MJ had already pushed the buzzer. A nurse came through the door as MJ was disconnecting the monitor.

"Whoa, in a hurry, are we?" The nurse said with a smile. "Doctor said you'd probably be able to leave today. I'll give him a buzz and make it official." She picked up the phone and dialed. They couldn't hear what she said, but she turned with a smile and gave them thumbs up. She hung up the phone and pushed Jeff out the door. "I'll help her get dressed, you wait outside."

Jeff let himself be led out the door.

Jeff and MJ stopped by Captain Harris's office to let MJ give more details on the men that attack her at the auditorium. MJ was back to her old self. She was anxious to help catch the crew that was causing all the trouble.

"MJ! You look marvelous!" John Harris had on his best smile as he held his arms out to MJ. She came over and gave him a hug. "Thanks John, you are sweet."

Jeff and MJ took chairs in front of Harris's desk. MJ knew the drill. She gave Harris all the details of the attack, where the men were hiding, how the attack took place and how they managed to take out Roger and Kelly and herself. When she finished, she suggested a crime scene artist so she could have them draw a portrait of the attackers.

Harris took her to an interview room where she met up with the artist. Jeff and Harris went back to his office.

"Donnie gave us some good clues about where he was being held. He did a wonderful job of describing the ride to the place and the ride from it, when they released him. Even though he was blindfolded, he remembers details about it. He has an acute sense of hearing, and that sense was enhanced when the put the blindfold on him." Harris handed Jeff a folder with several sheets of paper inside. Jeff opened it and began reading. It was Donnie's description of his kidnapping.

"First thing I remember is the big guy in front that zapped Kelly. They were both big guys. Roger was zapped right after Kelly, then MJ, and finally Krug. I think MJ could have possibly taken them out if Krug hadn't fallen on top of her. She didn't have a chance after that." Jeff continued to read the rest of the document. It was three pages of a very detailed description of the vehicle, the building and the men. His statement about the argument and the result of it left no doubt that the one time leader was out of the picture. They had been careful about using names, but he had heard the names, 'Arquet' and 'Carter' used, along with nicknames for some of the others, such as 'Butch', 'Samson' and 'Skinny'. He was sure that 'Arquet' was no longer a factor, and that 'Carter' had taken over as the leader of the group.

His description of the building is what held Jeff's attention. The details about coming in on a concrete floor, then going up a metal stairway, to a second floor that was a wooden floor was very detailed. Donnie's sense of direction had not been diminished by the blindfold. He recanted each turn, approximately how long between turns, and his sense of how fast they had been moving. It was an amazing recall of the entire scenario.

Jeff handed the folder back to Harris. "Wow, that's great. Have you been able to figure out where Donnie was held?"

Harris took the folder and slipped it back in his file. "We have some ideas." He pulled a map of the city out of his desk drawer and laid it out on the desktop.

Jeff stood up and they both leaned over the map. Harris picked up a pencil and began his explanation.

"We have the definite starting point, here at the coliseum." He pointed with the pencil. "Then if Donnie's sense of direction is correct, they took off this way," He followed a street on the map with the pencil tip. "They evidently were going pretty fast, then they got on the freeway bypass about here." He pointed again. "Donnie thinks they were probably driving about the speed limit by then, so as not to attract attention. According to his memory, they drove for no more than ten minutes, then exited the freeway to the right; down an exit ramp and then they must have stopped at a traffic light, as he recalls they sat there for almost a minute before turning left."

Harris turned the map a little so they could see where he thought they had stopped. "This point here and the junction of East 33rd street and Langley Boulevard match that description. It's close to the industrial park that used to be part of the car parts factory here." He pointed to a location on the map. Jeff remembered the factory. It had been closed for almost ten years now.

"If he was in that area, it would figure. There are quite a few abandoned buildings there that are empty. Donnie described the gravel parking lot, and he said there was a slight echo when the car doors were closed. He thought that indicated some kind of a solid fence. His description of sounds is phenomenal. He says it's from being a musician. He has an ear for sounds, and noises."

Jeff looked up at Harris. "If he's right, they might still be there. They wouldn't have any suspicion that Donnie could figure all that out from the short time that he was there."

"Right and his description of the ride before they turned him loose help to confirm that area. He says they drove on city streets until they got to the bus terminal. He figured the direction of travel, how many turns, and where they stopped. It almost has to be that area there." He pointed with the pencil, jabbing the map.

"So what's the plan?" Jeff sat back in his chair.

"What plan?" MJ had returned. She sat in the chair next to Jeff and placed a hand on his arm.

"We think we may know where the gang is located." Harris said, pointing at the map. "Donnie had a tremendous recall of details about his abduction. We think we may have the area located."

MJ looked at the two of them. "That's great! Let's go get these assholes! I've got a score to settle."

Harris grinned, "Hey MJ, how do you really feel about them?"

MJ was looking at the map. "Where is it?"

Harris pointed. "We have some unmarked cars driving the area. We've got the main routes in and out covered. Anybody coming out of there is going to be stopped and questioned. Once we are sure of the exact location, we're sending in a SWAT team."

"I'd like to be on that!" MJ and Jeff had the same response simultaneously. They looked at each other, and then did a high five.

Harris held his hands up. "Whoa, whoa! That ain't going to happen. You two are officially civilians. No way could we let you go in."

MJ and Jeff argued for awhile, then finally conceded the liability was too much for the department to take responsibility for. Captain Harris did say he would allow them to be on the scene when the arrest went down, and they would have an opportunity to watch the proceedings from the surveillance van.

Harris thanked them for their concerns and the information they had been able to provide, and even more for the assistance in recovering the weapons that had been hijacked. He ushered them out of the office and headed to the squad room. He would meet with the chief and the various commanders that would be forming the task force.

MJ and Jeff decided to head back to the office and see how the recovery of the weapons had gone. Jeff kept looking over at MJ. She appeared to have completely recovered from the effects of the taser and stun gun attack. She would catch him looking at her and give him a reassuring smile and squeeze on the arm.

They parked in front of the office and walked in past an empty front desk. They could hear voices coming from the central station, so they headed back there. The door was open and Marty was standing in the open door, talking to Bobby.

"I saw you driving up and I knew you'd want to get all the details from Bobby." She held the door for them. "I'm going back up front. Betsy and I will hold the fort." MJ looked questioningly at Jeff. "Betsy?"

Jeff grinned. "The Mossberg 12 gauge." He explained. MJ nodded and gave Marty thumbs up. Marty returned the gesture and headed to the front office. MJ turned to Bobby. "Congratulations Bobby. Sounds to me like you need to hit the boss up for a raise." Bobby looked up and waved at MJ. "It worked out pretty well, if I do say so myself." He gave Jeff a jab in the ribs. "Yes, I'll be looking for a fat bonus check, for sure!" Bobby turned back towards the console. The map was still on the display, and the blips were still showing on the screen.

"The Feds made the bust." Bobby pointed at the flashing icons. "They took one of the boxes out of the trailer and opened it. My tracker was still transmitting."

"The agent in charge there called back a little bit ago, they have four suspects in custody and are trying to figure out how they can return the shipment. Evidence and all that, you know."

Jeff gave MJ a hug. "As long as we know we'll get it back, I'm sure Erikson will be very happy."

MJ spoke up, "He should be, the shipment wasn't really under our contract for security. Whoever had that contract ought to be really, really happy."

Jeff agreed, "We come out smelling like a rose, thanks to Bobby. We might even get an expanded role in the security."

Marty called back from the front desk. "Erikson, the man, is on the phone. Wants to talk to you, Jeff."

Jeff grinned at MJ and Bobby. "Told ya." He headed to the front desk.

"Hunter here." Jeff said into the phone.

"Yes, Jeff, just wanted to let you know how pleased we were with the outcome of that hijacking. That could have been a disaster for our company."

"Glad we could help. It was our tech's idea. Bobby Cantor had the manufacturer install our tracking beacons, just to be on the safe side."

"Well, give my thanks to Bobby. And be sure to give him a little extra in the paycheck. I'll be more than happy to foot the bill for that."

"Thank you, Mr. Erikson, we planned on doing that anyway."

"My treat, and when you get a chance, stop by my office. I think we might have to modify our contract. You and your company have shown great initiative and I'm impressed."

"Thank you, Mr. Erikson. I'll call and make an appointment tomorrow. As you've probably heard, there are several other events occupying our time right now."

"I've heard, and I understand. I have complete confidence that you'll do an excellent job. See you soon."

Erikson hung up, and Jeff told Marty to make an appointment with Erikson as soon as they got everything under control. He went back to the control room to give the news to MJ and Bobby. Things were looking up. Now if Harris could just pinpoint the gangs' hangout.

Chapter 41

MJ was getting ready to head to the auditorium for Rebel Yells' concert. Kelly had called in and said that he and Roger were already on site and that everything was cool. They had a sellout crowd. News of the kidnapping had been a big boost in ticket sales. Krug had checked himself out of the hospital and was there for the opening. Donnie's release had been like a shot in the arm for him. He had recovered in record time.

Jeff drove MJ to the convention center. Her car was still parked there. They promised to keep in touch, MJ with the reports of the concert, and Jeff with reports from Captain Harris. They kissed and hugged and waved goodbyes'.

Jeff was on his way back to the office when his cell phone rang. Much as he hated being on the cell phone when driving, he decided to take this call when he saw it was from Harris.

"What's up Cap?"

"We think we've got it." Harris said. Jeff could hear radio chatter in the background. We've set up a command post and we're getting ready to execute a search warrant."

"Where are you?"

"We've set up the command post in the parking lot of the old Boulevard Tire Store at East 33rd street and Langley Boulevard. You know where that is?"

"Heading there now." Jeff flipped the phone closed and made a hard right, heading towards the on ramp of the interstate bypass.

Chapter 42

Carter had an uneasy feeling. He should have heard from the drivers with the weapons by now. They were supposed to check in every time they crossed a state border. There had been no word for several hours and they should be out of Kansas by now.

He walked over to the window that looked out over the parking lot. Nothing new there. He looked at the boxes that contained the diamonds. Maybe he should hide them somewhere, at least get them out of plain sight. The boxes were sitting on the desk. He opened the first one and gazed in at the glitter of the loose diamonds inside. He reached in and picked up a small handful. He rolled them around on his palm, watching how they picked up the light and reflected it. He stuck the handful in his pants pocket. Just a little insurance.

Chapter 43

Jeff pulled around behind the tire shop. There were several marked and unmarked cars parked there, along with a SWAT van and a large panel van that Jeff recognized as the command center van. It had numerous antennas situated on the rooftop. It was black with dark windows. Jeff was directed to a parking spot near the rear of the building by a uniformed officer. Evidently Captain Harris had given the word that he was o.k. He got out of the car and walked over to the command vehicle.

He knocked on the panel door, and it was opened by a detective he knew by sight. The detective nodded and motioned Jeff inside the van. Captain Harris was sitting in a chair in front of a console. There were small monitors clustered over a shelf, along with receivers and other instruments that Jeff didn't recognize. A technician occupied the other chair. Jeff sat on a bench that ran down the opposite side of the van.

Captain Harris turned to Jeff. "We've run thermal imaging on the building. We're getting images of several bodies on the second floor. There is also an image of two more on the first floor." He pointed to the screen that showed the building in question. "Quite a bit of activity for an abandoned building, don't you think?"

Jeff did think. "Have you done any aerial surveillance?"

"We did a quick flyover with one of the Lifeline helicopters. There is nothing visible on the rooftop."

"That's good. That means they have to have vehicles on the ground if they're going to try to bust out." Jeff pointed at the building again, "Do you have any views from the other sides? Any vehicles been spotted yet?"

"We've done a complete recon of the area. There aren't any vehicles near the building. There are doors that are big enough to allow a truck to enter. We're assuming the car or cars are parked inside."

"Good assumption. Do you plan on making an assault? Or are you just going to go to the door and knock." Jeff was serious. If it was just maintenance people inside, it wouldn't do to make their presence known. He doubted seriously that that was the case. He felt, as he thought Captain Harris felt, that the people they were after were the one's occupying the building.

"We're doing some more surveillance. They aren't going anywhere, and if they try, we'll intercept them before they can go ten feet." Harris was listening to his headphone. He turned and motioned to one of the techs and was talking to someone on the radio.

"We're picking up some conversation from inside the building. It's not clear enough to know what they're saying, but from the tone, it doesn't appear that they've been alerted."

The monitors had three views on display. One of the Techs was switching so that the display showed different sides of the building. The must have had cameras set up all around the perimeter of the building. The views were sharp and clear. The cameras had pan, tilt, and zoom capability, so they could focus on any portion of the exterior that they wanted.

There were several overhead doors on the street side of the building. These were the doors that the vehicles probably used for access. Besides those, there were at least four more doors that Jeff counted that were ordinary access doors for pedestrian traffic.

Harris pointed at the view of the street side camera. "You can see vehicle tracks leading to and from those bay doors. Those have to be recent. It appears there has been quite a bit of traffic in and out of the building."

They sat in the van, watching the building as reports came in concerning traffic in the area. They couldn't hold off for long. The media would be finding out about the road blocks pretty soon.

Chapter 44

Carter was on full alert. No contact from the weapons crew. He gathered together the remaining four members of the gang in the office.

"Something's up guys." Carter began, "The crew on the semis hasn't reported back, and they are way overdue. I think we might have been blown. I want you to start looking sharp. We may have been found out."

He sat the boxes of diamonds on the desktop. He had a coffee cup sitting on the table next to them. "I want each of you to take a cup of diamonds and put them in your pockets. If we have to make a run for it, it will be each man for himself. Might as well get something out of this."

The men lined up and took turns dipping out a cup of diamonds. When they were done, the boxes were empty. Carter had taken a turn also, in addition to the ones he had already taken. He figured he was more or less the leader and was entitled to.

"I think we'd be smart to split up. We've got three vehicles downstairs. Sort yourselves out however you want. When you get clear, you'd be smart to get out of the state. If you get stopped, try to split up. It makes it harder for the cops to chase more than one at a time." He looked at the four. Two of them were brothers, so he knew they would stick together. That left a total of four, including himself, to take the other two vehicles.

They trooped out of the office and downstairs. As they passed a window, Carter saw a large black van approaching. He hit the switches for the overhead doors.

"SWAT coming! Take off!" They all ran downstairs and jumped into the vehicles, the two brothers getting in the lead car. As they pulled out of the building, they could see more vehicles coming up, both marked and unmarked police cars. The brothers took off in the opposite direction of the SWAT van and were immediately blocked in by two patrol cars. Police in riot gear had them surrounded with shotguns at the ready. One of the other cars managed to get around the blockade and had made it about a half a block when it was stopped by another pair of squad cars. It too was immediately surrounded.

Carter had stepped back when the others were getting in the cars. It was apparent the cops had them surrounded. He ran to the other side of the garage and cautiously peered out the glass in the door. He couldn't see anyone near. He eased the door open and walked slowly to the end of the building. There was a crowd of police around the last car. The cars had all been stopped. Carter headed the other way. He went through a break in the fence surrounding the property and hurried around the neighboring building. He kept looking around, making sure no one was watching him.

There was never much foot traffic in this part of town. There wasn't even any sidewalk. It was an industrial area and usually all traffic was vehicular. Carter kept to the buildings, easing from one to another until he was two blocks away from the police activity. He came to East 33rd street and walked to the convenience store on the corner. He entered the store and got a cup of coffee. He paid for the coffee and saw a pay phone by the door. There was an ad for a cab company by the phone. He made the call and went over to the magazines to occupy some time until the cab arrived. He might get out of this yet.

Chapter 45

Captain Harris had his men round up all the prisoners and get them loaded in the paddy wagon. Jeff was standing by, trying to keep out of the way while the round up was going on.

"Did you get them all?" He asked Harris when there was a break in the action.

"I've got men checking out the building now. It appears they got spooked somehow. Maybe the truckers with the weapons called in or something. They all had diamonds in their pockets."

Jeff was pleased. If they could get all the diamonds back, this whole mess would be resolved.

"None of them are talking. They've all lawyered up. I'll bet you a buck there isn't a clean one in the bunch. They've all been through the routine before."

Just then Harris's radio came alive. He pulled the speaker/mike from his vest and listened. Jeff couldn't make out what the traffic was. Harris responded, "10-4, be right there." He turned to Jeff. "They found a body in the garage area. Got three bullet holes in it. Two in the chest and one right between the eyes."

Harris headed for the garage. Jeff tagged along, staying behind Harris. He didn't want to get accused of messing up a crime scene. He planned on just staying close enough to see what was going on.

Inside the garage, two officers, dressed in their black assault uniforms, stood over a body that apparently had been wrapped in a tarp. The body was lying on its back, hands crossed over its chest. A black automatic pistol was still in one hand. Harris gave them a nod and approached the body. He bent over and looked closely avoiding touching the body or the tarp.

"Better get the M.E. or the coroner out here. No doubt he's dead; it looks like the back of his head is missing." Harris was rubbing his bald head again. He looked back at Jeff.

"I think I know this guy." He pointed at the body.

"I'll have to wait for a positive I.D., but I think it's Bugsy Arquet. He used to be a small time hood around here. I busted him a couple of times when I was in the VICAP unit. After he served a stretch in the state pen, he moved to Detroit. I heard he hooked up with an outfit there."

"Looks like he came in second place in a gunfight." Jeff pointed to the automatic in the corpse's hand.

"No big loss, but I wonder who the winner was." Harris walked back over to the two officers to give them their instructions.

"Don't let anybody in this area until the M.E. gets here. We'll have a crime scene team take a look too. I doubt he was shot here. Looks like they were going to take him out and dump him someplace."

The older of the two, a sergeant, looked at the body, then turned to Harris. "Isn't that Bugsy?"

Harris nodded. "I think so, sure looks like him."

The sergeant smiled. "Always thought he'd end up like this, always was a punk."

Harris nodded. He and Jeff headed up the stairs to the second floor where another team was checking the rooms. Harris had received an all clear call on the radio. As they got to the top of the stairs, an officer beckoned to them from the doorway of one of the rooms. They walked to the room and peered inside. There were two empty boxes and a coffee cup sitting on a desk.

"I recognize those boxes." Jeff said, "That's what Jacobs uses to ship their diamonds in."

Harris led them back out of the room. "Seal this room for the crime scene team. We'll need to dust everything for prints."

"Yo boss." The officer closed the door and put a seal over the jam.

Jeff followed Harris through the rest of the building. There wasn't much else to see. There were some fast food wrappers and empty take out cups in some of the wastebaskets. No luggage or any other sign of occupancy in any of the rooms.

"Looks like this was their command center. They must have been staying in motels, probably near here. We'll have to check them out, see if there is anything else we can pick up. Might be some stuff from some of the burglaries stashed in one of them."

By this time, the media vans had shown up. Jeff could see reporters and cameramen trying to get into the lot. The officers had the area pretty well blocked off. The reporters and their crews were milling around outside of the barricades.

Harris took a deep breath. "Guess I'd better go down and make a statement to the wolves."

Jeff went downstairs with Harris. He headed outside the barricades towards his car when Harris met with the reporters. He wanted to give MJ a call and give her the news. Harris would want her to come to the station to see if she could identify her attackers from the crew that had been arrested. Jeff wound his way around the patrol cars and the increasing number of news vans. He got to the corner of East 33rd and headed back to the office.

He decided he'd stop and get a coffee before he went back. There was a convenience store right here on the corner. Jeff pulled into the parking and went inside the store. There was an old van parked at the edge of the building, probably belonged to the store clerk.

The store was empty except for a clerk behind the counter and a customer by the magazine rack. He went over to the coffee machine and got himself a cup to go.

As he paid for his coffee, the clerk spoke to him.

"What's going on down at the old car parts plant?" He handed Jeff his change. "First, I saw a bunch of cop cars, and now there's a bunch of news vans heading down that way."

"Dunno," Jeff said, not wanting to say any more than necessary. Wasn't his position to talk about it, at least until after it was on the news. He glanced over at the customer, who was apparently deeply interested in the magazines. He turned away from Jeff when Jeff looked at him.

When the customer turned, Jeff saw the butt of a pistol stuck in the man's belt. Jeff picked up his change and walked out the door to his car. He pulled his cell phone as he got in.

"Harris, this is Jeff. I'm at the convenience store down here on East 33rd. There's a man inside with a gun stuck in his belt."

Jeff heard Harris bark some commands to somebody, then he was back on the line.

"He didn't see me. It looks like he's waiting for somebody or something. I'd bet he's part of the gang."

"You stick in your car. I've got two squads on the way now." Harris was talking to someone else in the background. "I can't get away from here right now. I'm giving you to Lieutenant Mitchell. Stay on the line with him until the squads get there."

Jeff described the scene to Mitchell. As he was talking, he saw a cab coming down the street towards the convenience store. "Uh oh, cabs coming."

The man inside the store saw the cab coming too. He put his magazine back on the shelf and walked outside the store, a cup of coffee in a takeout cup in his hand.

Jeff wanted to grab his pistol and stop the man, but he knew how foolish that was. He updated Mitchell and looked back up East 33rd. He saw a squad car approaching at high speed and the man was getting in the cab. The cab had pulled in nose first into a parking slot. He was two slots over from Jeff. Jeff put his car in reverse and backed out of his spot. He pulled over behind the cab and stopped the car. At least the cab couldn't back up or move as long as Jeff's car had him blocked in. Jeff took the keys from the ignition, grabbed his pistol, just in case, then got out of the car and started walking towards the approaching police cars. He heard the cab door open and footsteps running towards him.

The man had his hand inside his jacket. Jeff could see that he intended to take Jeff hostage. The police cars were in plain view now, just a few seconds away. Jeff took off running towards them. The man stopped and ran back into the store.

Jeff thought he would probably try to take the clerk hostage. He turned back towards the store as the patrol cars screeched into the lot. The officers waved Jeff away and headed towards the door of the store at a crouch, guns at the ready.

Chapter 46

Carter had recognized Jeff when he walked into
the convenience store. He had seen him when they
were casing Hunter Security. He didn't think Jeff had
ever seen him. He turned away when Jeff came in the
store and faced the magazine rack. Where in the hell
was that cab?

He breathed a sigh of relief when Hunter left the
store. He saw the cab coming down the street, so he put
the magazine back on the rack and headed for the door.
He saw that Hunter was still parked in the lot, talking on
his cell phone. Hunter looked up when he walked out
the door. Carter avoided his look and headed for the
cab. He had just sat in the back seat, when he saw
Hunter back his car in behind the cab. Hunter had
recognized him. He saw the squad car coming down the
street. Had to move fast.

Carter got out of the cab and ran after Hunter
who was now on foot. He was grabbing his pistol when
he saw that the patrol cars were too close for him to
grab Hunter as a hostage. He turned and ran back into
the store. The clerk was standing behind the counter, his
mouth hanging open. He thought of using him for a

hostage, but there was only one way a hostage situation would be resolved, and that was with him in custody, or dead.

He had noticed a rear door when he had used the bathroom while waiting for the cab. He ran that way now. A quick glance over his shoulder told him that both police officers were approaching the front door of the convenience store, but cautiously. He slid out the back door and came back around the building until he could see the front of the store. Both officers were at the door, guns drawn. Hunter was squatted down behind his own car, with a cell phone in one hand and a pistol in the other.

Carter looked at the squad cars. They were parked side by side at the entrance of the parking lot. The lights were still flashing and the engines were still running. Both cars were empty. One man cars. Good! Carter ducked down low and headed for the police cars. The cab driver had gotten out of his cab and was kneeled down behind it, his hands over his head, as if that would protect him. Hunter and the police were focused on the front door. Carter eased over to the nearest patrol car. The driver's door was slightly open. Nobody noticed him move to the cars as the old van that was closest to him was blocking their view of that side of the building. Carter made the short dash to the patrol car. He slid into the driver's seat, keeping his head down below the level of the windshield. He had the car in gear and was moving before anybody noticed him. A shot was fired, hitting the side mirror on the passenger side. Carter drove past the other patrol car and slowed long enough to put a shot into the front tire as he passed. He slowed again and did the same thing to Hunter's car. Then he hit the accelerator and tore out of the parking lot, lights still flashing. Two more shots rang out and he heard one hit the car.

Carter was hitting sixty when he passed the intersection with the boulevard. An oncoming car hit its brakes and was rear-ended by another car. Carter swerved around them and kept going. He headed for the city. He had to find someplace to switch vehicles, and fast. The chatter was constant on the radio; there were more vehicles in pursuit.

He saw a Wal-Mart just ahead. He swung into the parking lot and jammed on the brakes. He left the police car with its lights still on and motor running. He ran towards the store, stuffing his pistol in the back of his pants under his jacket. A few people stopped and stared at him, and one man yelled at him, calling him a 'stupid cop!' Carter paid them no attention. As he neared the store, he slowed to a walk. People weren't watching him anymore; they were looking at the police car with the lights flashing. They probably figured that somebody had been caught shoplifting.

He saw a woman getting into an SUV. She put some packages in the backseat, then got out her keys and headed towards the driver's door. Carter kept moving towards her as she opened the door. As he came up along side of her, he reached into his coat pocket and pulled out a stun gun. He gave her a shot to the back of the neck and as she was falling, he took the keys from her hand. He pulled her twitching body over between two cars parked in the adjoining row and lay her down. He walked back to the SUV and got in the driver's seat. He had to move it back to make room for his legs, then he started the car and drove slowly out of the lot, leaving just as two patrol cars came screaming up to the lot and pulled in by the still running squad car he had just left. He drove slowly for two more blocks on the side street, then headed out towards the freeway.

201

Chapter 47

Jeff had changed his flat tire. The patrol officers had left together in their car after changing their flat. The shaken cab driver had left as soon as his cab was clear. There were a couple of detectives interviewing the store clerk. The cameras in the store had caught most of the action and the detectives confiscated the tapes and were going to have copies made of the pictures of the man that had been in the store.

Jeff went back to the site of the raid. Captain Harris had gone back to the station and left Lieutenant Mitchell in charge. Jeff gave Mitchell his take on the suspect at the convenience center. They were in agreement that he was probably part of the gang. Mitchell told Jeff about finding the abandoned cruiser and the apparent getaway. The lady in the parking lot had given them the description of her SUV. They had an all points lookout for it now, but Mitchell didn't have a lot of hope in recovering it soon, there were too many SUV's with that description on the road now.

Jeff promised to keep in touch, then headed out to try to make it back to the office again.

Chapter 48

MJ was backstage. She was watching Donnie do his thing out on the stage. There was a packed house. The news of his kidnapping had escalated the ticket sales for his performance tonight. She was caught up in the music, enjoying herself in spite of all that had been going on. This made a good break. She looked to the opposite side of the stage. Kelly and Roger were there watching too. They both glanced up at MJ and gave her a thumbs up. They were having a good time also. After all that had happened, they were all in pretty good shape. The effects of the stun guns and tasers had worn off.

As if to counter the good feelings, MJ's cell phone buzzed against her hip. She had it fastened to her belt and set on vibrate. She pulled it off and looked at the screen, it was from Jeff. He wouldn't call unless it was important; he knew she didn't like to take calls while she was working. She pressed the talk key "What's up lover?"

Jeff updated her quickly on the events of the afternoon. He let her know that Harris would want her to come down and see if she could identify her attackers from the group they had arrested.

"Harris will want to talk to Roger and Kelly too." Jeff continued, "He knows you're all working tonight, but touch base with him when you can, o.k?"

"Sure, I'll get with Kelly and Roger and we'll figure out the soonest we can all get down to the station. How're you doing?"

"I'm fine, a little frustrated that the last guy got away. They're still searching for him. We recovered most of the diamonds, but I'm assuming he has the remainder that's still missing."

"Hang in there. It ain't over 'til it's over." MJ gave him a kiss over the phone, then they disconnected.

She watched the rest of the show, then when they took a break, she headed over to the side where Roger and Kelly were standing by. Donnie was with them, obviously in a good mood.

MJ filled them all in on the latest. Roger and Kelly were both happy they had made the arrests and recovered almost all of the stolen property. They made an appointment with MJ to meet at the office in the morning so they could all go over to the PD and check out the suspects that were being held there.

MJ called Captain Harris's office and left word that they would be coming by in the morning. According to the aide that answered the phone, they were still processing the crew that had been arrested. They had identified all of them. They all had priors. MJ had figured as much. She left her contact information with the aide and hung up. They still had to finish the show tonight and escort the crew back to the hotel. There was a post show celebration planned to take place at the hotel later. She and the boys would be attending that also as part of the job.

Chapter 49

Carter had dumped the SUV at the mall. He had caught a cab back to the motel he was staying at. He went directly to his room and started packing his gear. He didn't have much, so it didn't take long. He transferred the diamonds from his pockets to his laptop bag. He reloaded his pistol and put it in the bag too. The stun gun he kept in his jacket pocket. His car was parked in the lot close to the room. He had checked in with a fake I.D. and so he checked out and paid up. He wanted to keep the I.D. clean.

The job had turned into a bust. At least the crew that Arquet had picked didn't include any of Carters associates. That had bothered him at first, but now he was glad. None of the bunch had known Carters real name. He had used the Carter identity before, but now it was probably burnt. If anybody talked, they'd put Arquet's death on Carter. He didn't care, there wouldn't be any other link back to him. He had been extremely careful from the start. He had these super thin latex gloves that he wore whenever he was on a job. He was also very careful about leaving anything that would have his DNA on it. He'd have to dump his pistol. No big problem, when he got back to his base, he could replace it. He'd hang onto it for now, just in case.

He put his gear in the back seat of the car, his laptop case on the passenger seat. He put the car in gear and headed for the freeway.

Twenty miles down the road, Carter pulled into a rest stop. He waited until the restroom was empty, then went up to the mirror. He hung his jacket up and pulled off his shirt. Underneath, he was wearing a padded vest that gave him a little paunch and more size to his upper body. He put the vest in an overnight bag at his feet. He placed a small case on the sink in front of him and then looking in the mirror, he began removing his heavy eyebrows. They peeled off and he put them in a plastic bag. He pulled off his wig to reveal a neatly shaved head. The wig and the bag went into his case. He pulled some rolls of cotton out of his cheeks and threw them in the waste can. He rinsed his mouth with a mouthwash and flexed his lips. Working carefully, he started working on his nose. When he was finished, he had a small roll of flesh colored putty in his hand. He tossed it up and caught it, then put it in a plastic bag and dropped it in the case also. The last change he made was to remove the contact lenses that made his eyes black. He put them in their own contact case and then put the contacts in the case on the sink. The case went into the overnight bag with the vest and padding. He put some eye drops in his eyes, blinked his now light blue eyes, and smiled at his reflection.

He examined his new look in the mirror. A leaner, tougher looking face looked back at him. He splashed some water on his face and ran his hands over his head. Grabbing some paper towels, he wiped himself dry, then picked up his overnight bag and headed back out to his car.

He drove off. Any video's that had captured him back there would be of no use now. He'd have to get a new look for his next job. He thought of the diamonds in his laptop bag. He smiled. The job had been a disaster, but still, he could afford a new look.

Chapter 50

MJ, Jeff and Kelly and Roger were all standing in Captain Harris's office. Harris had the documentation for each of the prisoners on his desk. They had gone over the papers together, and since they all knew what the score was, all that remained was for MJ and Kelly and Roger to make a formal identification of the men that had attacked them. They had already picked them out from the photos, but Harris wanted to do a lineup and have each of them pick them out from what Harris had determined to be something that the prosecutor could run with. They decided MJ would go first, as she was the last one to go down at the attack. Kelly and Roger would get their turn as they had been incapacitated through most of the attack.

They all walked down to the lineup viewing room. MJ went in first with Harris, and the rest waited outside in the hall. MJ took a seat behind the one-way glass as the suspects were brought in to the viewing area. Harris had populated the lineup with some officers and employees of the department along with the actual suspects.

MJ had no problem. She pointed out all three men. She was positive, and Harris noted that fact. She was dismissed, and Kelly and Roger were brought in one by one. They both identified their attackers successfully. Harris was pleased; the lineup had been a success. Not one mistaken identity and each one was one of the crew they had arrested at the warehouse.

They all adjourned to the break room. They gathered around a table, with Harris sitting at the head.

"Good job!" He looked at his friends sitting at the table. "You identified the very ones I had picked out. The prosecutor is going to be very happy with this information."

MJ, Kelly and Roger exchanged a high five over the table. Jeff sat back and watched. It appeared all of the cases, including most of the recent burglaries were going to be resolved. The only one missing was the one they called 'Carter'. Arquet's body had been formally identified through his fingerprints. It was assumed that he was the ringleader and Carter was something like a lieutenant, or second in command. His status was still a mystery. Nobody so far had talked. Harris planned on trying to interview each one of the men he had picked up individually, to see if any would try to plea bargain. Since they all had asked for lawyers, it didn't look too promising. He hoped that when the prosecutor made an offer for charging them with a lesser offense if they cooperated, they would see the light and fill them in on what they only now suspected.

The kidnapping, and it was still a kidnapping, even though they had released their prey, had the most severe penalty. It would be a big bargaining point in the discussions. Harris had high hopes that one of them would break and fill them in.

As far as Carter went, the only thing they had to go on was a few video shots, and the name. Somehow, they couldn't find any physical evidence to try to find his real identity. Harris thought that was because Carter was a real pro, and not just your run of the mill crook. It would have been nice if he had left at least one fingerprint, or a hair, or something they could get a DNA sample from. They still had no idea where he had been staying even. They had run his picture to most of the motels in the area. So far, nothing had turned up. Even if they did get a hit, chances are the room had been cleaned by now and evidence would be hard to come by.

211

Finally, they were all finished at the PD. Kelly and Roger headed home for some much needed rest. They still had another concert to attend, and then they would have to escort Rebel Yell to the airport for their departure. MJ and Jeff headed back to the office. Jeff wanted to bring the crew up to date on the latest proceedings and assure them that the worse was over. They still had to maintain a sharp lookout. Even though they were almost absolutely certain that Carter had left the area, they didn't want to take a chance that he might still possibly show up and create more mischief.

Chapter 51

Jeff and MJ were finally alone back at the house. They had court appearances being lined up and more statements to file, but the whole escapade seemed to be over.

"I still wonder about the guy called 'Carter'", Jeff said, pulling off his shirt. He threw the shirt in the clothes hamper and squeezed past Mj, who was leaning over the bathroom sink, brushing her teeth. She hummed something at him and he gave her a pat on the rear as he headed for the bedroom.

He pulled out an old Iowa State sweatshirt and pulled it over his head. He headed for the kitchen.

MJ came out of the bathroom wearing a long flannel robe. Damn! She looked gorgeous no matter what she wore. He smiled at her and pointed to his drink.

"Want one?" She nodded and he made her a Manhattan. He speared two cherries and put them in the drink and carried hers and his Vodka and 7up to the living room to join her on the couch.

They clinked glasses and settled back on the couch, propping their feet on the coffee table. Neither spoke for awhile, sipping from their drinks and relaxing.

"What a deal!" Jeff finally spoke, putting his arm around MJ.

"Thank God that's over" She said, moving a little closer to Jeff.

"Yes, now we can get down to the important stuff.   When are we getting married?"

The End

Proof

Made in the USA
Charleston, SC
18 July 2011